"Fred"

By C.J. Corey

Contents :
- Acknowledgments and Dedications
- Forward
- Land History

Chapter 1 - New Beginnings
Chapter 2 - The First Scare
Chapter 3 - It Is Real
Chapter 4 - Father Oscar
Chapter 5 - The Kids
Chapter 6 - Shadows
Chapter 7 - Up Close
Chapter 8 - Mediums
Chapter 9 - Fathers Oscars Helper
Chapter 10 - Hates Change
Chapter 11 - The Dog
Chapter 12 - Proof
Chapter 13 - Attention
Chapter 14 - Jump
Chapter 15 - Footsteps
Chapter 16 - Here to stay
Chapter 17 - Others Recollections
Chapter 18 - Living Together

Acknowledgments

I have got to say a massive thank you to all my friends and family.
All four of my children and my beautiful grandbabies have had to live or put up with "FRED" over the years.
They have reminded me of things that I had forgotten and sent me their accounts of "Fred" over the last few months.
To my eldest son Billy for all the hard work in putting it all together and having so much patience with me. Thank You kiddo x
My Mum and Dad for always being there when times have gotten tough.
To my lovely neighbour Jo for always sitting with me and listening

when "Fred's" made an appearance.
To the lovely vicar and his acquaintances.

Also to William, the Author of The Lady In The Bay Window, who has given me so much help over the months, giving me the kickstart to have the courage to start writing, thank you.

Dedications

I dedicate this book to…

My lovely, beautiful Mum Maggie, one of the kindest, selfless ladies I know.
My Dad, William, My Hero, Our Hero. Everyone's go-to person.
The grandkids and great-grandkids also adore you both. Thank you for everything you both have done for me and my kids over the years, We would be lost without you both.

Forward

I have always been into the paranormal, always going on ghost hunts and visiting haunted hotels, like a certain well-known hotel in Northumberland numerous times. It is a place I would recommend ghost hunters to go visit.
For my 30th birthday, I took a coach full of friends to stay there, and what a laugh we had. We used the same coach driver every time; he became a good friend to all of us. He took us everywhere. He is a lovely man and laughs and jokes along with us on our travels, but I will never understand why he agrees to take us. He's scared of ghosts.
He is petrified of the unnatural. He used to stay over on long-distance trips, we would often see him

sitting alone at the bar, refusing point-blank to get involved in "our nonsense".

He once got so scared in one haunted location, that he ran along the landing banging on doors and waiting for someone to answer. He ended up in a room with six women and was more terrified than the rest of us! He got some right ribbing for doing that on the journey home; he took it all in his stride, a little embarrassed if nothing else.

I have stayed in York, done the ghost tours, and while others screamed, like my cousin Kerry, who gripped me so hard she peeled the skin on the top of my arm, leaving me bruised with her finger marks for days after, I mostly was the one that just used to laugh it off and never really believed it to be real. I was what you call a sceptic. Now though, my mind has done a 360 turn around and it has changed.

I used to occasionally put "Fred's" antics on my social media.

The picture of someone looking out from my son's bedroom caused a big reaction, so many messages, telling me again to write about what was happening in this house.

School Mums are intrigued, asking, "How can you live there?".

So that is why I thought I'd start writing about it all. Others always wanted to know about "Fred" and his antics.

Land History

A few people have done a little history on this house and the land it sits on.
There is a document that mentions it was built near old Quaker ground, Also there was a mine very nearby, so who knows if the tunneling went this far.
We could also see that the underground tunnels from many years ago from the castle that the Mary Queen of Scots and others used before her untimely death are extremely close to this house.
 A few years ago builders on this road uncovered an opening to one of these very old tunnels.

Another explanation that was given to us by a local Priest, was that in the olden days, if you were not baptised by the church and you sadly passed away, you could not be buried on the church grounds.

This caused some religious families to try and bury their loved ones as close to the church walls as possible. Leaving them in unmarked graves.
We live next to the church walls, we can clearly see the churchyard from our upstairs windows, plus there is another church across the road.
There have been so many theories over the years, but we are still no closer to actually finding out where "Fred" came from.

Chapter 1 - New Beginnings

We moved into this house the day before my 40th birthday. It was a cold November day. When we arrived in the early evening, we noticed that the dew on the grass in the front garden had frozen. When we finally got the keys to enter the house, it was painfully cold. It took us quite a few days to warm up the place properly, as it had been empty for over two years. Our family consisted of me, my husband Roger, my three teenage kids from a previous marriage, and our one-year-old baby, Jack. We'd been searching for a bigger home since I found out I was pregnant with Jack. Our old house had only three bedrooms, and I did not want to put a baby in a room with two teenagers, plus, there was no more room for an extra bed for him in there.

The first few months of house hunting were disappointing. None of the houses felt like "home." However, I had often walked past this particular house when my son Lee had played football at a field near the end of the cul-de-sac. I remember saying, "I would love to buy that house if it ever went up for sale." Looking back now, it's strange how much of a pull this house had on me. It was the only one I ever spoke about wanting in this particular area.

One cold April Sunday morning, while attending another of Lee's football matches on the same field where the house was, we bundled up with scarves and gloves, pushing Jack in his pram with the dreaded plastic cover he despised. He hated the cover so much, constantly pulling it up while we struggled to tie it down. We soon learned to plan our outings around his naps just to avoid the battle of the pram cover.

As we walked by the house on our way to the field, Roger suddenly pointed at the window and said, "Look, that house is up for sale!" Sure enough, through the rain, we saw a small for-sale sign in the window—no big wooden sign in the front yard like you would usually see, but an A4 piece of paper. We could not make out much detail due to the rain, so we continued to watch Lee in his football match. After two hours of standing on a rain-soaked field and chasing a muddy, hyperactive Jack, we headed back home along the road, shivering and soaked to the bone. As we passed the house again, the rain had eased off a little and I could read the sign more clearly. "Oh my God, it IS for sale!" I said to Roger, excitement bubbling up inside me. Lee, whose eyesight was so much better than mine or Rogers, started reading the numbers out for me to place into my phone and encouraged me to either call the number or knock on the door.

Without even thinking about it I walked down the driveway and knocked on the door, but no one answered yes. I was a little disappointed no one had come to the door but I returned up the path, saying, "Let's ask the other kids what they think first." And as I dialled the number that was given to me by Lee, I felt good. This house felt like the start of something new, something big. If only I had known then what I know now.

One phone call was all it took, and everything moved quickly from there. The kids were thrilled, and I couldn't wait to see the inside of the house. I visited the house for the first time with my dad while Roger was away for work. I didn't bring the kids—I wanted to make sure it suited our family before getting their hopes up.

From the moment I stepped inside the porch, I fell in love with it. The space was bright and airy, with large oak drawers and windows on either side of the front door. It felt welcoming, and I knew immediately that this would be our forever home. My dad, who had come along for support, agreed. The kitchen was three times the size of ours, the bedrooms were also so much larger than the rooms in our current house, and when the owner showed us the beautifully kept garden I could not help but smile; I imagined a kid's swing hanging from the tall conifer tree that was situated in the far right corner. The garden also was private, with no houses overlooking it—a major bonus compared to our current place which was like living in a fishbowl.

I did not hesitate. Without even calling Roger to tell him I wanted it, I turned to the homeowner and said, "I want it, It is just perfect for our family." She smiled, telling me they'd been waiting for a family to come to view it as it had been a family home from the start—they didn't want to sell it to just anyone; it had many happy memories here for them and I could see it was a battle for them to let it go, from that moment on we agreed it was to be ours.

However, selling our old house was a different story. It was a stressful few months of buyers pulling out at the last minute and endless house viewings. It became a nightmare. I hated people walking through our home, especially with their shoes on. It was a house we'd taken so much pride in, where my older three kids had grown up. Our very own memories of birthdays, Christmases, and even bringing Jack home from the hospital for the first time and showing him to the older kids, we had parties and family gatherings over the years and I knew it was going to be incredibly hard to let go of this home but we needed space, it just had to be done.

Some of the potential buyers were also incredibly rude, talking about tearing down walls or ripping things up. I found it so disrespectful that I refused their offers and some were above the asking price. Eventually, though, after what felt like a lifetime of people trudging through our home we found a buyer, and a "SOLD" sign finally went up.

Packing up our old house was an emotional rollercoaster. I'm a hoarder of memories—everything my kids had ever drawn, written, or worn over the years had been kept in boxes. Letting go of those things was hard, but Roger insisted we only take what we truly needed. We had weekend after weekend of clearing out old furniture and clothes and things I had kept hold of for absolutely no reason. Roger made multiple trips to the tip, often putting his foot down when I tried to hold on to something that hadn't seen the light of day in years. When the moving day finally arrived, the excitement was palpable. We had run into a problem as we were handing over the keys to the new owners of our old house early in the morning; we were left waiting in the cold for hours, as the keys to the new house weren't ready. By 5 pm, we were still freezing, sitting in cars and vans with all our belongings, waiting for the estate agent to show up. It was incredibly frustrating, and by the time we got inside the house, we were all at our wits' end cold and grumpy.

The house was dark, damp, and freezing, and we had black bags and boxes scattered everywhere. I was wondering where the hell to start when there was a knock at the door. We did not hear it at first, but the second time it happened, one of the kids heard it and rushed to see who it was. It was our new neighbours—one with a pizza and chips and the other with a bottle of wine and lagers and pop— they stood there asking if we were ok and welcoming us to the road with open arms, we asked if they would like to come inside but they kindly refused, seeing that we were in a bit of a state, not wanting to intrude.

I was so touched by their kindness after having such an horrendous day, that a lump had formed in my throat. I thanked them and they left us to it.

Fifteen years later, Jo, our next-door neighbour, is still one of my closest friends.

She's been my rock on more occasions than I can count, and our families have grown so close she and her husband are now like part of the family.

That night, after unpacking just the essentials, we all sat on the floor and enjoyed the food and drinks that had been kindly given to us. We were all at this stage exhausted, but happy to be in our new home.

As the night wound down, we eventually got the kids sorted, each in their new rooms, and I finally put Jack to bed. We had sold his cot in preparation for a new toddler bed, we hadn't had time to set it up yet, so he slept in his carrycot in our room. By the time I had a bath and climbed into bed, I was utterly exhausted, but there was a sense of peace. We were finally in our forever home.

I had taken two weeks off work to unpack and settle in, and with the help of my parents, the kids, and close family relatives, over the coming months, we eventually made the house ours. The move may have been an absolute nightmare filled with tears, lots of hard work, and many sleepless nights but in the end, it was worth it.

Chapter 2 - The First Scare

I wish I could remember exactly the dates as to when things first started happening here, but in those first few months—whilst I was trying to get things sorted and also getting used to the new sounds that a new house made, I didn't take much notice if keys went missing or a hairbrush wasn't where I'd left it the day before. I blamed Roger or the kids. They'd say it wasn't them or just ignore me or tell me I was losing my mind, and either an hour or two later, the items would turn up nowhere near where I'd left them. A few times, they would be in the same place on the rug in the room and turn up when there was no one else in the house.

Also now and then I'd catch a whiff of perfume or a smell of cigarettes, knowing it wasn't my perfume and none of us smoked.

Again, I put it down to the new surroundings. I had learned from my lovely neighbour Jo that the previous occupants had smoked, so I justified it by thinking the smell was probably lingering on the wallpaper, and until we had the chance to fully decorate every room I knew it was something that I would have to put up with for now. If doors slammed, it was just a draft. When the knocking started, I blamed it on the radiators or just the new house sounds—I had some kind of justification for most of the goings-on.

One of the first unexplainable things to have happened was when the older kids were at school, and I had Jack at home playing around my feet. I was sitting in a chair that had a pouffe attached to the side of it. I had placed this chair next to the open staircase facing the fireplace. We had a sofa next to the window with another two-seater next to the fireplace, where the TV sat on a black glass cabinet. The furniture fitted perfectly around the living room, and I thought it had started to look very cosy now with the family pictures up on the walls and my favourite ornaments on the shelves we had put up, and on the stone-built fireplace beam above the fire.

Jack had his toys lined up on top of the pouffe. He would pull himself up by it, stand there, and make his baby noises, playing quite contentedly, and I loved these moments by ourselves. It was rare with the older kids in and out and me working shifts; sometimes it felt like a train station here. I was just about to get his bottle ready as it would soon be his nap time when I saw him look up at the staircase. He was scowling, and then I saw his face change. You could visibly see something was bothering him. He then said in his baby babble, "No, no," he then turned and looked at me with his eyes wide, pointed up the stairs, and then just started to scream. He couldn't say many words at this point —he was about 18 / 20 months old. But the fear in his eyes and the way he said "no, no" and then the scream he let out after scared the hell out of me.

Quickly picking him up and looking up to where he had been pointing, there was nothing there. I said, "Jack! Look! nothing there, baby it's ok." But he buried his head into my neck and would not lift it back up.

I took him into the kitchen with me, stood, and cuddled him for a few minutes. He was sobbing gently into my neck at this stage and it took a lot of reassurance until he put his head back up, when I thought he had calmed down enough for me to place him in his high chair, I gave him some of his favourite snacks, hoping to take his mind off whatever had caused him to be upset like that. While getting his bottle ready I was spooked. Something did not feel right and it made me feel very uneasy. After giving him his bottle, I sat and cuddled him to sleep in the dining room, then placed him on the dinning room sofa so I could keep an eye on him also if I am going to be honest, I did not want to go up the stairs now, I then made myself busy by doing what needed to be done around the house—all the while trying to process what I had just witnessed and worried that maybe I was reading to much into this.

I did not go back into the dining room whilst he was sleeping, only to pick him up when he had woken from his nap, although I did keep popping my head around the archway to check he was ok.

I did not tell anyone what had happened until a few weeks later when the same thing happened again. This time, Jack was sitting there playing, and he looked up toward the staircase. His head shook from side to side as though he was saying no to something, he then put his hands over his eyes and started to whimper. I watched as his hands went over his eyes wondering what it was that he was seeing, so I got up from the sofa, scooped him up, and walked outside with him since it was a nice warm spring day. After the second incident, Jack wouldn't play near the stairs anymore. He would move his toys if I left them on the pouffe and take them across the room to the chair next to the fireplace.

In between these two incidents, what made me think something was going on in this house was when we put Jack into his bedroom. We had bought him a low Thomas the Tank Engine bed and decorated it lovingly for him with nice and bright colours, and he settled in fine, much to our delight. We installed safety gates at the top and bottom of the stairs for obvious reasons. These gates hadn't been in place for very long, and the older kids, instead of unlocking them, couldn't be bothered and started climbing over them, much to my annoyance. I was fed up with reminding them about it. One night I came home from work to find the top gate hanging off. I asked who had done this, and they all blamed each other as usual.

My dad is our fixer-upper, always has been, Thank God my dad was so good at everything; nothing would ever get done unless he came up and sorted it out for us. It was past 9 pm now, so the gate could not be reattached until Dad came up in the morning with his familiar tool bag. I would hear Jack trying to get out of his bed in the morning. His bed was on the floor with wooden boards raised around it in the shape of a train. The effort it took him to climb over the side was funny to watch because he was so noisy. He would knock and bang—we would hear huffs and puffs, then a thud when we knew he had gotten out of it, followed by him running along the landing into our room, knowing he would get picked up for his first-morning cuddle.

I knew that this morning, when he woke up, I would have to be more vigilant in case he went near the stairs, I had left the door wide open anyway, just in case, and since he normally always ran straight into our room, I hoped he would do that in the morning like he always had.

The next morning, I listened to the familiar sound of his banging and knocking and his struggle with trying to get out of his bed. I looked at the clock—it was 4:39 am. He was up early this morning; he would normally not wake until around 6-ish. I had just woken up myself and was laying looking at my mobile phone.

 I listened for him to get to the landing, ready to pick him up for his morning cuddle, but before he got to my door, I saw a white/blue light appear. At first, I thought it was light from a window or something but then it moved in a very strange way, kind of gliding so softly. It was long and had bright lines running through it. It was moving very gracefully. It then started to take on shape. It looked like it was taking on the shape of an arm. I was so fascinated by it, but for some reason, it did not scare me at all— there was no fear in me at this stage as it was beautiful and I was just staring, watching it take form, my eyes were frozen on it. It must have only been for a couple of seconds, but it had felt much longer.

Then, remembering that Jack was on his way to run into this light, I snapped out of my trance. Like I said it was only a second or two, but it felt much longer. The next minute, Jack came tottering along the landing towards the doorway, and I saw the bright light curve

around his shoulder as though to
guide him into our room. I saw it
take shape and I do not know if he
felt or even saw it but he did not
seem scared, Then it turned him
towards my room. He just turned
with it, and then it vanished—
totally vanished. There was nothing
there now, not one bit of light. It
was so dark; I jumped out of bed,
scooped him up, and put him in
between me and Roger. He was
not scared at all. I don't even think
he had noticed it; he was his
normal happy self. He was not
even phased by whatever it was
that had just made contact with
him. I, on the other hand, was in
shock. It took a few minutes to
process what I had just seen and
try to get my head around it.

I mustered up the courage to go downstairs to get Jack his morning drink, a change of nappie, and make myself and Roger a drink, then walked back up the staircase, keeping my head down all the way. On entering the bedroom I saw that Jack had now woken Roger up, I did not know whether to say something. They were playing peek-a-boo. I passed Roger his drink, gave Jack his, and got back into bed. Roger had not seen a thing; he had no idea what I had just witnessed. He was absolutely oblivious to what had just happened, and I didn't think he would believe me anyway. I was still doubting myself at this point, so again, I kept it to myself.

In the days after this, I convinced myself that if it was a spirit, it was not a bad spirit, as it was protecting my son from being in danger, especially near the stairs. I had to admit I was not scared at this point; I was actually intrigued. It did not seem like a dark entity—the colour had been so lovely and so bright. I have never seen that lovely bright light since, except for one time in my dream. I was having a nightmare that I still remember to this day. It was one of those dreams where you wake up feeling exhausted. In my dream, there was something very evil trying to take over my body and mind, and I was chanting the Lord's Prayer. In my dream, I say chanting, but I remember screaming at it—I was scared, so very scared. It looked like a big black shape; I knew it was something bad. I could feel it trying to get into my head when, all of a sudden, that beautiful bright light appeared. It immediately lifted the darkness and stood beside me. I felt like a weight had been lifted off me, and at that time in my dream, all the fear left me. I was no longer scared. It did not say anything, but I knew it was something good and then the dark thing just went—it disappeared. All that was left was a beautiful bright light, and then I woke up. That dream was so real, and I have only ever told two people about it, as it makes me sound like I am losing the plot. I was very scared that something bad could have happened had that beautiful light not come and saved me when it had, that same light that had guided my son into my bedroom.

Chapter 3 - IT IS REAL

It was one of those rare weekends off work for both of us, and we had spent the afternoon taking the kids out bowling. Once we got home, I set out the usual treats for our Saturday night tradition of pizza and a movie night. We finally agreed on a movie, and after everyone was bathed and showered, We put the film on while waiting for the pizza to arrive. Each of us was settled into the corners of the two sofas when Jack, who was almost three at the time, suddenly pointed toward the dining room and said, "Mummy, who's that man?"

We all froze. My eldest, Andy, asked, "What is he pointing at, Mum? There's nobody there." Lee had just gone upstairs to grab his dressing gown, but as soon as Jack spoke, he heard what he had said and he ran back down, so fast. Jack, still staring at the dining room, said, "He's gone now. The man's gone," then casually returned to watching the movie, as if nothing had happened.

The older kids looked at each other and began teasing each other, throwing out nervous oohs and aahs, followed by, "I'm not going in there tonight, Mum." I tried to calm everyone down, telling them that toddlers often see things that aren't there. But I don't think any of them believed me. For the rest of the night, whenever anyone needed something from the dining room, it was always me who had to go in and get it, None of them stepped foot in there until the next morning.

Fast forward to today — I now have two beautiful grandchildren, Grace and Gray, and Just a few weeks ago, my grandson Gray did something eerily similar. I managed to catch the end of it on my mobile phone. He was playing with his toys on the floor just under the archway lying on his side facing the dining room. His face suddenly was filled with fear, his eyes as wide as Jack's had once been. I could tell he had seen something. He got up quickly and sprinted towards me, jumping onto my lap. He was obviously unnerved by something, but he was a toddler and could not verbally tell me what it was. I sat and cuddled him for a few minutes until he had forgotten about it and went back to playing but he picked his dinosaurs up and came and placed them on the sofa next to me. It had happened in the same spot where Jack had seen "the man" years ago.

There's another video of Jack when he was about three.
 He was in the kitchen playing on his toy guitar, singing "Twinkle Twinkle." putting on a show, I was filming him, wanting to send the video to his Nannie Mag and Grandad.
I did not notice anything odd at the time, but my daughter Annie whilst showing her the video after school did. She pointed out what we call an "orb" floating past him. You can see Jack's eyes follow it, watching something that at the time was invisible to us, but when slowed

down you can see it very clearly. I've screenshotted the Orb and will let you see it for yourselves.

Orbs have become a common occurrence in photos and videos over the years. One video shows Jack dressed in his Harry costume for Halloween, he is waving a wand around in circles pretending to cast spells on us all, while orbs swirl around him.

 I've captured so many more orbs since then. One particular orb stands out—it was large and bright, moving slowly, very cleverly weaving in and out of the top of the banister of the stairs. It had a pale yellow colour with a dark spot in the centre. I was just laying in my bed early in the morning, not scared but mesmerised by the way it moved so I picked up my phone and recorded it. I am glad I did as I needed to show others that I was not making this stuff up but more importantly, I was not going mad.

These sightings have become part of my life now. I can usually tell when they're about to happen because the temperature drops dramatically, creating cold spots.
 The most common places are either in the living room or on the stairs landing just outside my bedroom door.
I've learned to quickly grab my mobile phone so I have the chance to catch as much evidence as possible and over the years that's exactly what I've done.
 There are the blue and white flashes, I don't like seeing them, they still unsettle me.

The first time I noticed them was about two years after we moved in, I was in bed, watching TV. It was a really cold winter, Jack and I were alone in the house since the older kids had their things going on. By this stage, they were now teenagers and were out and about coming in at all hours sometimes even after I had gone to bed, and tonight was one of those nights. Roger was working away as usual.

That night, something strange happened. As I lay in bed, I saw smoke coming from my mouth as I breathed, the radiators were on and It wasn't cold enough for this to be happening, Then a cold pocket of Ice hit me, It felt like the kind of cold you experience when you have to scrape ice off your car, when your gloves get soaked through, your fingers go numb and you blow on them hoping to get some warmth back but to no avail. I slowly pulled the quilt up further under my chin, but something urged me to feel the radiator beside me to check if it was working as it had gotten so cold, a small blue-white flash of light appeared, it flickered a few times then it gave off an electrical charge, like a shock— it went right at up from my fingertips to the palm of my hand then up to my elbow. I screamed, not out of pain, but literally from pure shock. I felt a tingling sensation travel up my arm, and there was a strange smell, almost like something burning or a welding smell.

The cold then vanished as quickly as it had appeared. I had never experienced anything like it before, and it terrified me. Really terrified me. That night, I slept with the lights on. It seemed that whatever this presence was; it knew when Roger and the kids were not at home. From then on it started to target me more when I was alone and it got to such a stage that I became scared and hated being on my own.

It had started to affect me now more than ever and I was becoming a nervous wreck and jumpy which I had not been before.

The next morning, I realised I could not ignore it any longer. These lights, flashes, and cold spots were becoming too frequent and frightening. I called my mum for advice. She told me I should have gotten help years ago, back when the first things had started happening. She was right, but how do you tell someone—anyone—that you think you have a ghost? That you are seeing lights and flashes? hearing voices? It sounds insane and I was worried that people would think I actually was insane.

My mind was now made up. I had reached my breaking point. That morning, I googled the local churches and found a number. I called half expecting to be laughed at or hung up on. Instead, the woman who answered was kind. She calmly told me I needed to speak to Father Oscar and gave me his direct number. I thanked her, relieved that I had not been ridiculed, and immediately after ending that call, I wavered over whether I should go ahead and call Father Oscar.

I finally gathered the courage to call him, but I put the phone down after the first couple of rings. My heart was racing. I had no idea how I was going to start this conversation. I was playing it over and over in my mind when the phone started to ring.

Picking up the call, I heard a voice say" Hello, can I help you"? He had reversed my call. His voice was soft, and he spoke to me calmly. This reassured me that I had made the right decision in contacting him. I did not reply straight away as my head was wondering how I was going to word this conversation.

"Hello, this is Father Oscar," he said.

I hesitated again for a moment before blurting out, "I think my house is haunted, I think I have a ghost." There it was—out in the open, it had left my mouth, and there was no going back now. I braced myself for the awkward pause of disbelief, snigger, or laughter.

But Father Oscar did not react in any of the ways I feared. Instead, his voice remained soft as he asked, "Can you please tell me what has been happening?".

I took a deep breath and began recounting everything—I was speaking amazingly fast trying to get as much information out as possible. I told him about the flashes of light, the cold spots, Jack's strange comments about "The man," the orbs we had also

been seeing. I explained how it had all started off, A little bit of knocking and things moving, but recently things had escalated.
I was feeling more frightened and uneasy than ever. I must have sounded like a raving lunatic but feeling better for being able to unload it all onto someone else.

When I had finished reeling off most of the things that I could remember, there was a moment of silence. I at first thought he had put the phone down on me, then Father Oscar spoke in a soft low tone. "It sounds like you are experiencing something very unusual, but I want you to know that you are not alone. These kinds of occurrences can happen, and they do happen, and they are more common than you think. Again, I will tell you that you are not alone, and yes, while they can be unsettling and cause distress, there are ways we can try to address them." Let me try to help you. He then suggested coming over to the house to do a blessing. "A house blessing can bring peace and calm and I can also try to help move the spirit on," he said. "But I would also like to talk with you and your family to better understand the situation. Sometimes there are things we don't see, but that doesn't mean we are helpless and cannot try and deal with them between ourselves."

Father Oscar to my relief did not seem sceptical or dismissive, and that gave me a big sense of relief. He assured me that whatever was happening in the home, we could deal with it together. We then set a time for him to visit later that week preferably when Jack was at school.

As I hung up the phone, I felt a strange mix of emotions. On the one hand, I was still terrified of what might be lurking in our home. I was scared that having a priest or Vicar in here could escalate the situation.
 A couple of my friends had scared me a little by telling me that they had heard that it could make things much worse, but on the other hand, knowing that Father Oscar was coming gave me a glimmer of hope. Maybe this could all finally be resolved, and "FRED" would be on his way.

Chapter 4 - FATHER OSCAR

Father Oscar's first visit left a lasting impression, and we became friends and someone I learned to trust. He had done these many times before. After finally mustering the courage to get help, I had thought that perhaps inviting a priest into the house for a blessing would put an end to the strange occurrences that had been a constant nightmare for me for so long. But what I did not anticipate was that things after his visit were about to take a turn for the worse and my previous concerns and friends' advice were unfortunately correct.

When Father Oscar arrived that day, he came in his full robes, carrying holy water, a cross, and some tea lights that I expected to be the guiding light into which "Fred" would go. It was a beautiful sunny spring afternoon, and though I had been so nervous all morning, I had managed to keep myself busy by scrubbing every inch of the house. I wanted everything to be spotless for his visit. I had made sure even the dining room table—my expensive dark oak six-seater that we had brought over from the old house that I had refused to part with—was polished to perfection.

I had not told anyone about Father Oscar's visit, not even my family. I did not want them to laugh at me or question my decision to get the house blessed. I just needed someone to do something to make me feel safe again.

Annie was not working that day and her boyfriend also had taken a day off work so they could have some time together. They were upstairs in her room, completely unaware of what was about to go on. I had tried to hint that I needed time alone, but they had not taken that hint, so I figured I would just play it by ear and see what they would say when he turned up. Jack, thankfully, was still at school, and Andy and Lee were at work, and college and would not be back until later that evening. Roger was yet again working away, So it was just me and Father O downstairs when he arrived.

As soon as he stepped in I saw him look straight up towards the top of the stairs, they were straight in front of you when you opened the front door. He stood, staring there for a few seconds but he did not say a word, He then walked into the living room before getting to work.

He said hello, then told me a little about what he was about to do. He then laid out a cloth on the dining table, set down three small white tea lights, and put his cross in front of them. I handed him some coasters, hoping he'd put his candles on them to protect the table, but he did not seem to catch on that I was passing him them to place the candles on and just placed them at the side of the table. He then lit the candles whilst doing the cross signs and did the Lord's prayer over them all. He gave me a leaflet and told me to say the prayer that was printed on it with him, We walked from room to room muttering the words that were on the pamphlet, He moved through the house with me on his heels, sprinkling holy water in every room it was thrown everywhere all over the windows and mirrors and I know this sounds so silly, but as he was doing this all I could think about was how long it had taken me that very morning to clean and polish them all.

I could see Annie peeking out from her room when we had got to the top of the stairs, wondering what the hell was going on, but she did not say a word, not one word, I could see she was trying not to laugh. I gave her a "you dare" look as he proceeded to make his way into her room. He nodded in her direction and carried on. He was still reciting prayers and throwing holy water all over her stuff. I was hoping that she would not come out with any snide remarks whilst he was doing this, and, to my surprise, she still never said one word, they both just stared at us. Father O then calmly told them that he would like them to come downstairs and be part of the blessing. They both quickly got up, never questioned him, still never saying one word, and they left the room and started to go downstairs, Both now obviously intrigued as to what was going on.

We then all gathered in the dining room. Father O had given Annie and her partner the same leaflet that he had earlier given me. After explaining to them what parts he wanted them to join in with, all the time he was looking at me in a bemused way and started to pray.

Still, neither of them had said a word yet. He then led us in a protection prayer.

I could tell Annie's partner was not quite sure what to make of it all; like I have said the looks and odd smirks at each other did not seem to bother Father O and he seemed to be well aware of their disbelief, still he did not say a word to them about this. Instead, he got them involved and explained step by step as to why and what he was doing. They started to take him seriously by the end of the prayers and the blessing.

He finally got to the end of the prayers and calmly told us to keep hold of the leaflet. Father O then assured us that things should now be calmer and more settled. He then gave me two crosses and asked me to place one in Jack's bedroom, as he felt he needed protection the most. I placed the other on the shelf next to the fireplace with the rosary beads my neighbour Jo had given me a few months ago — He stayed and started to give tips to us all about how we could now protect ourselves with prayer and the holy water and I must admit I was feeling very optimistic about the whole situation. We had all got a much-needed cup of tea at this stage and were all having a conversation about what had happened over the years when he stood up and announced that he had another appointment to get to, he started to gather his remaining items and doing one more cross with his hands on our foreheads, he made his way to the door.

The moment he left, I walked over to the dining table to clear the now burnt-out tea lights that he had lit for the blessing. That is when I saw it—the three white burn marks left by those three little candles, right on the surface of my pristine oak table. I was absolutely furious. After all my effort to keep everything perfect, my favourite piece of furniture was ruined!

I eventually had to replace the table as every time I cleaned it, the marks that the tea lights had made hit a nerve, much to the delight of my kids, who had been telling me to get something new and modern for a while.

To this day, whenever I bring up the burn marks, Father O just brushes it off. He never really addresses it, and though I laugh about it now, at the time I was fuming it had been an expensive table, But the real issue was not the table—it was what came after his visit. Instead of bringing peace, the house seemed to go up a few notches, and it seemed to rebel badly against the blessing.

As for "Fred," people often ask me where the name came from. It wasn't anything personal, just something I made up to avoid scaring the kids when they were younger. I did not want to keep saying "ghost" around them, so I called it "Fred" to make it less frightening. Now that they are older, they know the truth, plus we are so used to calling it that now that the name has stuck.

At the time, I had no idea that Fred—or whatever it was—was about to make its presence felt in ways we were not prepared for.

Chapter 5 - THE KIDS

The older kids had quite a few things happen when they were home. The boys were in their room laying in their beds talking away when the loft hatch lifted and just flew off. They were scared to death running from the room and refusing to go back in for a few hours.

Doors have opened by themselves, and there has been knocking on the walls and doors. Just typical "FRED" stuff, trivial things that now do not faze us anymore. We are used to it —we are hardcore, you could say.

One thing I remember well is when Lee was about 15. Andy had moved out by then, so Lee now had the back bedroom to himself.

One night, while we were all asleep, I woke up to the sound of a piercing scream followed by pounding footsteps across the landing. It was Lee, and he was so scared he was crying. He had jumped straight into our bed. I could feel he was shaking badly. Roger and I both sat up. I jumped out of my bed to turn the light on, to find out what had happened. He had woken the whole house up. All of us were awake now.

Annie yelled, "What the hell's going on?" and Jack started crying because Lee had run through his room screaming to get to ours.

Roger went to calm Jack down and try to get him back to sleep—it was only 4:42 a.m. Annie came into our room, not at all sympathetic, and called Lee a "GIRL!" before turning and going back to her room, not even asking what had happened. I asked Lee to tell me what was wrong. He was still visibly shaking, but finally, he said, "Mum, the workbench moved. It woke me up and I saw It was dragging along on the carpet, then I heard a groaning mum and I just ran out—it was horrible. That growl was so loud. I'm never staying in that room again."

That night, Lee ended up sleeping with me.

He was genuinely spooked.

The next morning I tried to rationalise it, thinking maybe the growl was a cat or a fox outside; it was a warm summer night, and we'd left the windows open. I tried to tell Lee this, but it still took a few days before he would go back into his room. I bought him a new nightlight, and eventually, he found the courage to go back in there.

Annie had her own experience. She once saw someone by her window, looking out toward the road. She screamed, and I ran in, thinking, *What now?* She was sitting up in bed with her lamp on, visibly shaken. She pointed to where she had seen him, saying, "Mum, I know what I saw, so do not try to tell me a story to make me think it was something else." I did try to reassure her, saying maybe it was just the shadow of a lamppost or a passing car, but she insisted that she had seen someone.

Tucking her back in and still telling her it was probably a shadow, she asked if she could keep her lamp on that night. Her night light from then on was always on.

Thinking back now, maybe this should have been the right time to get out. This was not fair to the kids. It is one thing for me to try to deal with it, but going after my kids was a different ball game.

Very, very recently, Jack did the same thing that Lee had done years ago.

It was freezing cold; the heating was on all day and night trying to get this house warm. It had been snowing the previous day, so it was a lot colder than usual.

A piercing scream, followed by running, obviously woke me, sitting bolt upright in bed and waiting to see what was about to greet me. I pressed the TV remote to get some light in the room. Jack was as pale as a ghost. He jumped into my bed, pulled the cover over him, and told me something had pulled his quilt off him. He was shaking, "Mum, please let's move." I hate that room.

There is absolutely nothing you can do, that is the worst part, As a mother, you cannot protect your kids from it. How can you fight fresh air?

We had been waiting in the Play area for him to be seen when a nurse I had worked with a few years ago spotted me, She came right over and started to ask me about "Fred", putting my finger to my lips so Jack would not hear us, I whispered a couple of his latest antics, she listened intrigued, then asked if she could come and do a session at our house, looking at her confused, I asked her what she had meant, She then told me she and a group she was involved in did spirit boxes and tried to communicate to the other side, "no thanks" I said, you don't have to live with the aftermath, with that we said our goodbyes and I went back to where Jack was playing.

Chapter 6 - SHADOWS

Sat drinking my morning cup of tea I was watching the TV when something caught the corner of my eye, I then heard someone plodding along the landing not light footsteps but heavy stomping as if in a hurry, I looked to see if Jack had gotten up early and said "Good morning" even though I knew I would be sending him back to bed, It was just after 4.30, a school day, so there was no way he was getting up at this time, there was no reply and thought to myself he could not have heard me, I waited for him to finish in the bathroom, I waited and waited then jumped out of bed and knocked on the bathroom door to see if he was ok, there was no light on but I had heard someone go in there, heard the footsteps and also seen a figure pass my door.

Putting the stairs light on, I whispered Jack's name but got no response. I then slowly opened the door, as if he had been on the toilet I did not want to embarrass him. The bathroom was empty. I thought for a second or two, was I just being silly?, had I imagined it? I went back to my bed doubting myself yet again.

Then I heard the flush go... Good Morning" Fred", grabbed my phone, ready to call my Dad. I saw it was 4.42 am.

We had just come back from holiday, having had a lovely break away. Myself, Roger, and Jack.

The dog had gone to my Mum and Dad's home,
 We were able to just relax, knowing he would be spoiled and looked after.

The first couple of nights back we were all too exhausted to notice if anything was happening but by the end of that first week back,
"FREDS" presence was very much felt, those familiar icy cold spots, seeing shadows darting about from the corner of my eyes.
Gray also saw something on the first sleepover since we got back from our holidays.
Grabbing his favorite bedtime book, he jumped onto his bed and we snuggled down, as I started to read to him I noticed his eyes looking behind me, He then looked at me with a frightened expression,

Looking behind me, then back to him, I watched as he pulled his blanket over his eyes and said in a whisper "Memar" I don't like it ".. cuddling him and not being able to say or do anything at this time, not wanting to frighten him further, so I just kicked his bedroom door closed.
I carried on reading his book to him, all the while keeping my voice as steady and calm as I could, there was no way I wanted my grandson to be scared at this house so doing hide and seek with his blanket and trying to take his mind off whatever he had just seen he happily joined in with the game.
After laying with him for some time and waiting until he had drifted off to sleep, I walked out of his bedroom.

I had left a little night light on his windowsill just in case he woke up in the night, turning round to give him one last check, seeing that he had drifted off, an icy cold wind shot straight through me, It made my hair move, looking back towards Gray's room from the top of the stairs I saw a shadow dart out of his doorway, It was so fast there was nothing I could do, It was tall and dark and it moved towards the bathroom, coming in my direction hitting me full on, the chill it gave me was nothing I had ever experienced before but what I do know is that it chilled me to the bone.

Grace and Jack were downstairs nattering away, oblivious to it all, not wanting to scare them, I said nothing.

My head was telling me to grab him, and take him downstairs with me, but then I realised it had already left his room he was fine now and sound asleep I carried on downstairs, I walked past the kids and into the kitchen and poured myself an exceptionally large wine.

Jo next door popped around the next morning, she had been feeding our fish whilst we had been away and had been putting the night light on for a couple of hours each night after tea so as to make it look like someone was in the house.
On one of these nights, she had gone to turn it back off, just after 10 pm like she had all week but on this particular night as she had walked in the door and as she did she heard something, not being

able to pinpoint what it was, but it unnerved her enough to quickly pull the door back shut and go back home. Apologising for leaving a light on all night. She came in early the next morning and switched it off, feeling braver when it was lighter outside and inside the house.

Electrical items have been a nightmare in this house. Nothing lasts very long. On returning from my holidays, "Fred" must have been angry with us.

That first night back after plugging in my hair dryer, I switched the on button on the handle. Within seconds It sparked, and then a big POP! sound. followed by smoke. I threw the hair dryer out of my hands and kicked the switch with my foot to turn the plug off.

Only had this for less than a month, I blamed the manufacturer, replacing this the next day from the shop I had bought it from, thankfully still having my warranty.

Two days later, I plugged the new hair dryer in, and the same thing happened. I was so frustrated. It was now late. There was no way I was going back to the shop and not want to go to bed with wet hair. I got the ironing board out, plugged the iron in, and BANG!!, that was now no good. These were two separate rooms so it could not be the sockets. I now knew "Fred" was on a roll, The new hair dryer and iron have survived a few weeks now. They are the same make as the others and I have plugged them into the same sockets with thank God, no more problems.

That first week back there were constant knocks, shadows, electrical problems, and the familiar cold breezes. I know "Fred" was angry with me.

Chapter 7 - UP CLOSE

This next episode is my number 1 top scare. It was the first time that I wanted us all to just pack up and leave. After this event I never, ever, want to feel like this again, to say it stays with me still to this day proves it really did traumatize and shake me up badly and I hate talking about it to anyone.

It was early, just after 4 am and I was on my own with Jack, who had now been moved to the bedroom above the garage, he was a teenager now and had wanted the larger bedroom, my grandkids now had the other rooms, They had now been decorated lovely for when they slept over, which was normally at the weekend. I had gone downstairs to make myself a coffee, All the while knowing that something was off, it had felt colder this morning, and sensing that it was going to be one of those days "FRED" was going to be active, but nothing prepared me for what he was about to do that morning, After making myself a drink I was coming back into my bedroom, finding the remote that had been kicked off the bed at some point in the night I put the T.V on, flicking through the channels, looking for something to watch. Sipping my coffee, noticing that there was smoke coming from my mug I blew it away, then noticing something from the corner of my eye to this day I wish that it had not caught my attention. If I just stayed downstairs for a few minutes longer, curiosity got the better of me and I stupidly looked up towards the bottom left side of my bed.

There is a double mirrored wardrobe that you can see the doorway to my bedroom and the top of the landing to the stairs.

My eyes followed the movement and on looking into those mirrors what I saw next shook me to the very core. My heart skipped a beat, and I thought I was going to throw up.

I saw what looked like a large, well-built man. He was tall and he filled the whole of my bedroom doorway; he had what looked like a covering over his head; it did not cover his face as it was not a balaclava but more like a hoodie. It went over his head, seeming to hang over his face, nearly touching his nose. Seeing the outline of his facial features but not being able to see

his eyes because of it, he also had a light brown colour, with a shimmering lighter brown glow around him. I sat frozen to the spot, absolutely scared stiff but still not able to take my eyes off him.
It could have only been just a few seconds I was sitting there but it felt a lot longer.
Moving in slow motion he took two steps, very slow steps like I have said fear had me glued to the spot and I could hear my heart thumping in my chest when all of a sudden snapping out of whatever trance-like state I was in, My senses kicked in and my inner voice shouted, "OMG I AM BEING BURGLED, THERE'S A MAN IN MY HOUSE, I'M ALL ALONE AND HE'S GOING TOWARDS JACKS ROOM!!!!". Again it must have been seconds but it had felt like

forever, then the protective mum in me kicked in and going into a total panic I looked around my bed to see if there was anything that could be used to defend us both, but I Couldn't see anything, there was nothing at all around my bed that I could use, god knows If there had been what was I thinking I could do, the man id just seen was enormous but still I jumped out of bed, My head was all over the place but thinking I'd throw the hot drink at him and thinking that surely would slow him down a little, I started running out of my bedroom, I was expecting to be in a full-blown scuffle with an intruder and was very frightened, shaking and scared to death.

Reaching the landing and looking for the intruder I realized that there was nobody there, there was nothing at all on there. My eyes were adjusting to the bedroom light I had flicked on when running out, giving me a little bit of comfort but not much.

Looking around to see if he had gone into any of the other bedrooms, I could see that the doors were still shut from last night, and so was Jack's. I knew for sure nobody had opened that door, his door was so hard to open, you had to give it a really big shove and push and that always made a banging noise, a noise we were all familiar with. I had not heard that noise, so that meant he had not got into their yet and that was a massive relief to me.

I just stood on the landing, shaking my legs like jelly and trying to figure out where he could have gone in just those few seconds.

There was no noise of anyone running down the stairs either, so I knew he had not gone downstairs. My head was doing somersaults and there was nowhere he could have gone in that short time.

Quickly running into the bathroom, I lifted the toilet seat and threw up.

Sitting on the side of the bath afterwards with the door wide open I did not know what my next move was going to be. There was a man in my house, but I did not know where he was. I left the phone on the side of my bed when running out of the room. God knows why it was not my first instinct to just pick it up and dial 999.

Looking back now my head just told me to stop him from going into Jack's bedroom. Still sitting there on the side of the bath, not daring to move or look out towards the landing, my body was still shaking. I dared not stand up; my legs were like jelly.

Looking back now I know I must have been in some kind of shock.

It felt like ages since I had run into that bathroom. My mind went over and over as to what I had just seen, knowing this time that there was no way this had not just happened, this was not my imagination, I definitely knew that there was no way I was going to be able to just ignore this event like I had done with previous happenings, this had taken things to a totally different level.

To this day after this incident, I can still see that figure and the way it had moved from one side of the door to the other. The thing that I do know now is that it had been real, and I had seen it, there was no floating light and it definitely was not a fast-darting shadow. It had shown me itself for the very first time, it had been big and tall and had scared the hell out of me. Eventually plucking up the courage to come out of the bathroom and keeping my head down towards the floor so as not to see "FRED" again, my hands felt for the light switch, switching it quickly. I looked around again.

Knowing that I was going to have to go now and check on Jack to make sure he had not got into that room, I plucked up the nerve to open his door and was comforted to hear the loud noise it created in doing so.

Walking in I very happily saw that he was still, thankfully, sound asleep.

The dog, who had been laid with him was also fast on, his paws were up in the air and his tongue was hanging out of the side of his mouth and this made me smile, he also was fast on, coming into the room I had woken him up, Quickly he flipped himself back onto his paws, jumped down off the bed and went running onto the landing. Shutting Jack's bedroom door, I then went into the other bedrooms, even checking under the beds, behind the doors, and in the wardrobes. The downstairs was the next place to search and just like the upstairs that also was empty, I now knew that there was nobody in the house.

I went back upstairs, walking along the landing and purposely leaving the lights on, I went back into my bedroom and got back into bed.

Still do not dare to look up, especially keeping my eyes away from those mirrors.

My body started to shake, and it all hit me, I then burst out crying.

It had all been too much this time, being on my own had left me feeling extremely vulnerable and very frightened plus this time he had shown himself to me. I needed to call my Mum and Dad.

Reaching over to the right side of my bed where my phone had been on charge all night I grabbed it and pressed the side and the time popped up …. it was 4.56 am which meant that this had happened at around 4.40 am.

Poor mum and dad got another call at silly am yet again, and as always after calming me down they told me to go get Jack, get in the car, and go straight down to theirs, for

the first time in ages I was so very close to going but on already checking on Jack five minutes earlier and seeing that he was still fast asleep, Id not wanted for him to be disturbed or be affected by any of this.
The sky was now starting to lighten up and knowing that nobody was in the house I declined.
Just after 7 am that morning the doorbell rang and on opening the door I was so happy to see my Mum and Dad standing there.

When you hear people say ghosts float, this one did not, I actually saw it take a stride, it took two steps and moved very slowly but surely.
 The glow it had around its outline was so bright, and I cannot explain

this any other way than to say it was like glitter.

It had been cold when I had gone to make a drink earlier that morning but not like the cold I had experienced before when it sometimes did things. There had not been any smoke coming out of my mouth, no sudden cold breezes, So I had absolutely no idea that this was going to happen.

It had caught me totally off guard this time.

For the rest of the day, I was walking around in a zombie-like state. Replaying the moment in my head over and over.

When you experience something like that, it stays with you, I can still see that thing as it walks past. The way it took those steps like a normal person, the colour that it had around it, a light brown top half

with a glow. Never in my life do I want to be that scared again.
The thing I did now know was that something had to be done to get rid of him and it had to be done fast.
There was absolutely no way I ever wanted to experience anything like that again so that morning I was on the phone to the vicarage again, begging for Father Oscar to please come and help us.
He came out the very next day and tried to calm me down.
 He went around the house doing what he always did but this time I noticed he was reciting some different prayers; we both knew that no matter what he did "Fred" would still be here when he left, and it would be me that had to keep dealing with him.

Chapter 8 - Mediums

The first time I visited a spiritual group was with my mum, just a few weeks after my Nannan Mary passed away. We were heartbroken. Nan had been the glue that held our family together. With her twelve children, she was our rock. Everyone missed her terribly, so my auntie and mum suggested after seeing a flyer in a shop window we visit a spiritual church nearby. It was a small, unassuming building a little bit like a bungalow, It was a five-minute walk from my mum's. It had advertised that it cost just one pound for entry, and you got a cup of tea and a biscuit. The tea and biscuits were the selling point for me.

Inside, chairs were arranged in a semicircle in the centre, with six seats at the front for what we now know was for the medium speakers. There was a faint buzz of conversation from the regular attendees that had all gathered together. As soon as we walked in, a lady who I found out later was called Doreen approached me, smiling warmly. She immediately just came out with it and told me she could see lambs around me and just blurted out, "You're having a baby." I laughed … I DON'T THINK SO!, I said ... .No, she said it's true you wait and see, it symbolises new life. With a four-year-old boy and a three-year-old girl, the last thing I expected was another child, and I certainly did not want any more children at this stage.

Doreen was not deterred and said, "I see four children in your life. I can see three boys and one girl. I see blue." I was still very sceptical, but the moment felt surreal. My mum and auntie looked at me and shrugged. They then sat in seats with me towards the back of the building. We were trying to hide in the back. We had come not expecting anything and we were just intrigued to see how things transpired. The circle began with prayers and blessings.

Soon after the readings started as soon as they had started, a different medium stood up and pointed directly at me and I looked behind me to see if there was anyone else she could be pointing to. She then asked me, "Who has been going in the bins for cutlery?" My jaw dropped. A few weeks earlier, just after my Nan had passed, I had gone through the bins at her house to retrieve her old cutlery that had been accidentally discarded—pieces I had given her from the cutlery firm I had worked at years before. They were precious to me as I had bought special items, especially for her, I couldn't believe this woman knew something so specific and private, nobody could have known this and I had never seen this lady before in my life, plus we had turned up out of the blue. My mum, the only person who had seen me do it, squeezed my leg in absolute shock.

The medium then said my Nan was standing behind us, her hands on my mum's and auntie's shoulders, giving them flowers as a symbol of love. We left the session speechless and a few tears lighter, and a few weeks later, I found out I was 12 weeks pregnant with my son Lee. Doreen had been right after all.

This had all happened well before I had moved into this house and after having three children and going to work I just got on with life living in two different homes over the next twelve years.

Things at home grew even stranger. Following a house blessing by Father O, we had a few weeks of peace, but soon the activity ramped up again. Despite his advice against bringing a medium into the house, I knew I needed to. I began researching mediums and found one that had been highly recommended. I was cautious and didn't give him much information—only my mobile number and the general area we lived in. He called me back within an hour. I was quite surprised by this. He agreed to come over.

He asked me to meet him at the church up the road from our house so he wouldn't know my exact address until moments before his visit. This was to assure me he hadn't researched me or the house. When he arrived, I noticed he was a handsome man, neatly dressed in a brown overcoat and scarf. After shaking my hand and stepping inside, he immediately said, "Oh, I see what's going on here. You've got a man here, and your Nannan Mary is telling him to bugger off! She's here protecting you all."

I was stunned. I had not told him my Nan's name or mentioned anything about the spirit in the house. He said she was giving me flowers and wagging her finger, just like the medium at the spiritual church had said. He asked if I had run into the bathroom during the incident with a whispering voice. Again, how could he have known that? I had not mentioned the bathroom or the voice in my ear to him at all.

The medium confronted the spirit, telling him repeatedly that it was no longer his land, but the spirit refused to budge. My Nan, however, was still there, protecting us. The medium asked who Maggie was and said my Nan wanted to give her a message. Maggie is my mum's name. He explained that when Mum had felt down recently; it was Nan who had knocked over a picture frame in her bedroom. The frame was heart-shaped and held Nan's photo. This was another thing he couldn't possibly have known.

I told my mum about the medium's visit and asked if a picture of Nan had fallen recently. Mum teared up, confirming that a few days earlier, Nan's picture had indeed toppled off her TV cabinet when she had been feeling low. She had replaced it with an oval frame, but the old one had been heart-shaped, just as the medium described. The knowledge that Nan was still watching over us brought me and my mum some comfort.

He pointed his thumb toward Jo's house next door and said, who keeps saying this is the house that Jack built? I could not believe this as that was exactly what she had said years ago.
The finger wagged towards the bottom of the garden next. He built that wall and where has the greenhouse gone? I seriously could not believe what he was saying, as there was not one photo of the old greenhouse that used to stand where he was pointing. We had pulled it down the first week of moving in. As with Lee playing

football and Jack starting to walk, we saw it as a danger.

The medium also told me to confront the spirit like a naughty child, shouting at him to get out of the house. He admitted he couldn't move the spirit on entirely, but he promised that if things got worse, I could call him again. As he left, he reassured me that my Nan was not backing down—she was still giving the spirit "both barrels" for not leaving.
I felt a bit better knowing I was not alone in this fight, even if the fight was not over yet.

When I went to collect Jack from my parents, I told Mum everything the medium had said. She was comforted by the thought of Nan still being with us and shed a few tears knowing that she had been there when she had been feeling low and was now, watching over and protecting her and her family.

Looking back, I now believe it was my Nan's presence that had guided Jack safely into my bedroom when the stair gate broke. That peaceful light I had seen on the landing—warm, protective—was her. She was always watching over us and knowing that gave me strength in the face of all the strange and frightening things happening in our home.

"FRED" has been seen numerous times by different people, including me. Sometimes he is in the master bedroom, other times in the box room or the window above the garage. My mum, our neighbour Jo, and even other family members have seen him. Once, someone reported seeing a hand pull back the living room curtain while we were on holiday, but when they checked, there was no one there, and the house was locked.

There were three times when we pulled up into the driveway and saw "FRED" looking out at us from the window. The first time, I squinted, trying to convince myself it was a glare from the sun or a kids' toy. But he was just standing there, looking right at me. I was so unnerved that I asked our neighbours, Mick and Jo, to come in with me to make sure there was nobody inside before letting the kids go in.

We went room by room, calling out, "Is anyone home?" but found no one in.

Jo stayed with me until I got the kids and the groceries from the car.

Since that day, it's become somewhat "normal" to see "FRED" watching out onto the street, as if keeping an eye on the world.

We even captured a picture of him once. He was standing at the window above the garage, looking out at me and Gray whilst we were in the garden. He looked like he was watching my grandson play, Gray was in the sandpit with not a care in the world. "Fred" just stood there, not moving, for a couple of minutes—just enough time for me to take the photo.

I thought that by the time it would take me to get my phone out and be able to catch him, he would be gone, like previous sightings. It is strangely satisfying to have this picture as proof . Showing family and friends this capture was also validating for me as the photo I had taken after shows that he is not there, we have had hecklers ask if it is a light shade but there is no light shade up at the moment as Jack jumped up and knocked a piece off his original one so we had to take it down to replace which I also took a picture of to try and justify my capture. Taking a picture from the same spot on different days has also been tried but "Fred" seems to have gone camera-shy since then.

Another time, I was at work when I got an urgent phone call. I was with a patient when the receptionist, who knew me well, asked if I could take a call—she thought it was one of my kids. I picked up, and it was Lee, he was hysterical, screaming for me to come home. Jo, my neighbour, was trying to calm him down in the background. I asked to speak to Jo, and she explained that Lee had run into their house in his boxer shorts, as white as a sheet, shaking and crying. He had come home from school, let himself in, and went upstairs to change for football practice. I had laid out his kit on his bed so he could get straight into it. But as he was changing, he had heard banging sounds coming from what he thought was Annie's room. He thought that maybe she had come home, without him noticing, so he opened her door. As he did, he heard a moaning or groaning sound coming from her wardrobe, It was then followed by another loud bang. Terrified, he bolted out of the house and ran straight into Jo and Micks.

It turned out Annie had snuck in and knew that Lee had not heard her enter the house and then hatched up a plan, to scare Lee. She had then hidden herself in the wardrobe and made the sounds that he had heard. After getting the desired results and laughing to herself she then heard Jo coming back into the house shouting at "Fred", She jumped back into the wardrobes scared of getting herself a roasting from Jo, Later, months later she finally plucked up the

113

courage to confess to Jo, saying she knew she'd gone too far, she was scared by the way Jo had given "Fred" the what far. Not long after this, those wardrobe doors started to make real knocking and banging and also opened on their own, Annie it seems had given good ole "Fred" an idea so it had backfired on her as from then on her wardrobes became the main focus in the years to come.

One night, I was woken up by strange noises coming from Jack's room. By this point, Jack had moved into Annie's old room, as she was now settled with her boyfriend Bob. I thought he was having a nightmare, all I could hear at this point was muffled sounds but somehow knew something was not quite right, call it a mother's instinct. Getting up to check on him. We had always left his door open and with his nightlight on, as I walked into his room I saw him floating above his bed, stiff as a board. It was just for a split second, trying to adjust my eyes and trying to take in what I was seeing. His body dropped back down onto his bed, and I heard him land on the mattress springs and it made a noise, he then started screaming. I quickly scooped him up, rushed him into our room, and woke Roger. Jack sobbed, saying, "Mummy, it wouldn't let me shout for you. I tried hard, but it would not let me." Trying to calm him down and get my head around what I had just seen, we told him it was all a bad dream, he was having none of it and just kept repeating over and over that he had screamed for me but "IT" had not let him. He fell asleep with us that night and a few nights after he was about seven years old and this time it had affected him badly. He started following me around like a puppy after this event. Knowing after seeing this we needed to get help.

Nightmares had become more regular around this time. The ones where you are running but don't seem to get anywhere, the thing that was chasing me I never actually saw but the growling sounds it made as it was coming for me were enough to scare anyone. It always was just as it was about to get me, just about to pounce,a nd then I would wake up in a cold sweat, visibly shaken. The days after these nightmares, I would be exhausted.

Chapter 9 - Father Oscars Helper

This time Father O fetched a man that he introduced as a DR. I have forgotten his name now but I will call him Dylan in this chapter.

Father O turned up just before 10 am. He came dressed in a shirt, jeans and trainers. He was very casual, I think he now knew that it did not matter what he wore anymore "FRED" did not care he was here to see if it was all in my head. They had not said that but I just knew, if I'm totally honest I was a little ticked off with this approach, especially with Father O for fetching him as he had witnessed his activity in the house himself and I'd thought that we were better friends than that.

I had asked Jo next door to be here, I had told her what had happened and as always she was here to support me, we all sat down and over tea and biscuits I told them what had happened, He asked me about how it had affected me over the years and I told him that this time the event had shaken me up and that I did know that I never wanted to see "FRED" again. Then we told him about so many of the events that had happened in the past, he nodded and seemed to be taking it all in, he had a pen and notepad and was jotting things down. I thought to myself "he thinks I have lost the plot, he thinks I should be locked up".

I was exhausted and knew I looked shocked, Not being able to sleep after what had happened.

Having already gone around the house earlier doing my cleansing, sprinkling the holy water, and saying the prayer that he had given me on a leaflet the previous visit, Jo next door had fetched me her mother's rosary beads and a picture of Mary that had been blessed by a Catholic priest hoping that this may give us comfort or ward it away, at this point I was willing to accept anything.

When we had finished talking and drank our cup of tea, he then gave us all a sheet of paper with quite a few prayers and verses on it. This time the prayer he wanted us to recite was different. It seemed that he was going to go around this time with a different approach.

He had fetched a cross like always, he then blessed it then asked us all to give it a kiss. Saying some kind of protection prayer he went and blessed each of us. This time was not at all the same as his previous visits, I think he was trying to be more aggressive towards whatever was in the house, He meant business this time round.

When he had finished downstairs we made our way towards the staircase, Dylan and Jo followed Father O up the stairs and we went straight into Jack's old bedroom, on looking around to make sure Jo was ok I saw Dylan turn and look back towards the landing, he took a couple of steps backward then put out his hand and said to Jo, "do you feel that? "We all went to where he was saying it was cold, we stuck our hands out, Then I said," Yes it's always cold there, that's where I saw him, That's the door I saw him walking past".

Then that familiar cold breeze went past us all, making Jo's hair move as though to say "Yes I'm here "I then saw Dylan and Jo look at each other, both of them not quite knowing what to say next. Dylan then told Father O that he was going to go back downstairs and Jo followed quickly behind him. Both then started talking about what they had just experienced, Myself and Father O stayed upstairs and finished the blessings. When the house had been fully blessed and he had put his kit back in his bag, we sat and had another cup of tea, I then asked Dylan outright "Do you think it is all in my head then? Please be honest with me, as if it is I can at least go get some help _"he replied, "I will be totally honest with you, I will say you have a very active home and no it is not in your head, You need to get someone else in here to help you, what is on your stairs is not good and I would not like to live with it".

On the way out of the door, he turned to me and said "I think we will phone someone who can come out and move this spirit on, but I have to go above the vicarage, someone higher has to come out and do this."

I was so glad he had taken it all seriously, and that finally, we may, after all these years, get rid of "Fred" and get some peace. It had caused serious damage mentally to me this time so on hearing this I was elated.

We never saw or heard from Dylan again.

One night whilst reading a book, a cup of tea in one hand and the book in the other, I felt the bed suddenly shake. It was not a big shake but knowing it wasn't me spiked my curiosity. Thinking the dog had jumped on to the bed, I looked down towards the area. There was nothing there, so I put it down to me being engrossed in the book and probably moving without noticing. A few minutes passed and my right leg right down to my ankle went icy cold, putting my tea and book down I started rubbing my leg to get it warm, while doing this I noticed my icy breath coming out of my mouth, my stomach did a little flip and a feeling of nausea washed over me.

The start of these episodes always made me skip a heartbeat and I was scared because you never knew what was about to come next.

Shouting at whatever this was to Bugger off, Jack came running into the bedroom asking why I was shouting at him, not realising that he was in earshot at the time I told him that I was sorry but I was not shouting at him but was shouting at the book; it was a horrible book, and I had not liked the person in it. He looked at me like I had gone mad but not wanting him to be scared. This had been the better option, yes, I would rather him think I was crazy than have him scared.

He trotted back off to his room and I then realised the cold had gone; I was so happy at this, you seriously need to experience these breezes to be able to understand that feeling of complete and utter dread that washes over you not knowing what is coming next.

Picking up my book and drinking what was left of my cup of tea I went back to my reading.

We decided at this stage that Father O would have to come out for yet another visit.

This time when he came to the door there was a young man with him. The young man was in his late teens and was standing hopping from foot to foot looking extremely nervous, he gave me a little smile and introduced himself. Father O explained that he was from the parish and had wanted to learn about the paranormal, he was going to be sent somewhere so he could study how to deal with the unexplained.

Feeling a little sorry for this man knowing that this was going to be his first experience of any kind in the paranormal, I worried that by how he was pulling at his hands and awkwardly moving from foot to foot it may be too much for him and secretly hoped for the first time that "Fred" would not make himself known today.

I offered him a drink hoping that this would make him feel more relaxed, but the poor nervous young man politely declined.

Father O waved for him to come over and start the prayers with him, all the while explaining what he was doing and why he was doing it.

I had explained earlier on the phone about all the latest antics, but nothing had been mentioned about any of them in front of me, so I just took it for granted that Father O had given him a history of our house and "Fred."

This was not the case, I found out later, that this poor man had not a clue about "Fred" or the house.

Climbing the stairs to start blessing the bedrooms he carried on reciting the prayers and seemed to have got into the zone with Father O, so far nothing untoward had happened, on following them upstairs, all three of us were now on the landing. He had just started to walk towards one of the bedrooms when. SLAM!!!.

My grandson's bedroom door slammed shut on us all. Looking toward the man, I saw his face freeze in terror. He looked petrified.

Trying to keep calm myself I gently put my hand on his arm and asked him if he was ok. He nodded and gave me that same nervous smile.

Turning towards the bedroom door and nervously glancing at me Father O barged his way through, all the while saying a prayer and sprinkling holy water everywhere, myself and his companion hot on his heels, he did every corner of that room he blessed both sides of the door and then on his way out placed a crucifix above it, we turned to go back down the stairs and heard the crucifix fall to the floor, not one of us went back at that moment to pick it up.

Needless to say, I never saw that young man again.

Sometimes after these visits, I am left alone in the house and I am more scared of the after-effects than before, Jo is a godsend for this as she either comes and sits with me and chats until the kids or Roger comes home to take over.

Chapter 10 - "FRED" HATES CHANGE

I have tried to put the scariest events in this book, I call them my top 5.
These events have left me scared and completely unnerved for days after and they are embedded into my head, even today.
I have mentioned that we had a new kitchen and we also had the porch refitted with new windows and doors as I was trying to stop "them draughts", I had asked Jo to pop around, I had bought a bottle of wine, and wanted to show off my new porch, they had been fitted that week and I was so pleased with them, In she came and after pouring us both a drink I was

asking her what she thought about it all, She was saying how much she loved them and we started chatting away, putting the world to rights, moaning about the kids and the normal chit chat you have when the outside door opened, then the handle of the inside door pushed itself down then also opened as wide as it could, we just turned round and looked at each other in disbelief, I then said,"I take it FRED" does not like the change and we both nervously laughed.

It was a lovely warm night. After letting the dog out for a few minutes and making sure all the doors and windows downstairs were locked. I came up to bed, today had been a terribly busy day and sleep would come easy to me tonight, or so I thought. I had a bit of a thing with the doors and would lock them and then try to open them again, just to make sure they really were locked.

We had just had new patio doors fitted in the week before and I was making sure they were securely locked. I actually tried them 3 times to make sure I had locked them correctly; I was on my own with Jack again so was more vigilant than normal. Putting my tv on and checking that Jack had turned his gaming off which thankfully had, he was already asleep so on shutting his door I made my way back to my bed.

I must have dropped off straight away because when I woke up the tv was still on but the program I had been watching had finished and was now just on the home page, I squinted at my phone and saw it was just after 4am, I fumbled around the side of the bed and found the remote, turning off the tv then laid back down, I was shattered, I needed to go back to sleep and whilst laying there I could hear a strange noise it was like someone trying to open a door, I had not gotten used to the new door sounds yet so these squeaks were not familiar to me, what I did know is that the new kitchen doors had a squeak like it when you pushed the handle down and that was the same squeak I was now hearing, I thought "omg someone's trying to get in" I jumped out of bed and looked out of the window, I could not see anything, the windows were open and dad had put me security lights at either side of the doors just a few days ago and they were not lit up but I could still hear something messing with the handles, I went and put the light on thinking that if someone was trying to get in then this would send them running, it was getting lighter now and I kept looking out but nobody was there, the noises were still happening, at this point I was wondering what should I do, knowing that I would not settle until it had checked properly I knew I'd have to go myself, putting every light on as I walked out of the bedroom.

Picking up my phone on the way out I punched 999 and had my finger over the call button, just to be safe.

I first stood in the living room, straining my eyes trying to see through into the kitchen, there were double doors between the kitchen and the dining room and I had

bolted them shut last night as I always did before coming up to bed, now stood with the light on in the living room all I could see through the glass was my own reflection, all the time thinking "nobody would be stupid enough to still try breaking in now".
I walked into the dining room and switched those lights on as well. Unbolting the dining room doors and putting my hand round the corner feeling for the light switch. I flicked it on and could not believe my eyes. The patio doors were wide open, there was nobody there and our back garden was private, there was a gate that we had put in years ago that connected us to Jo's garden so she or myself could pop around when I was sitting in the garden. We were surrounded by a high fence on the opposite side,

plus we had also put a brick wall with a fence on the top at the bottom for more privacy. I could not understand how this had happened. I knew that I had locked them, I checked both doors to see if there were any marks on them in case anyone had forced them open with a tool but there was nothing. Pulling them back together and locking them both separately again I walked back upstairs, I doubted myself, so I started to mutter away, calling myself all names, and blaming myself for not locking the doors properly.

Getting back into bed, still angry with myself I left the TV on. What had just happened had unnerved me so it was more for my peace of mind than anything else, laying back down and still mad with myself, going over and over how I had messed up not locking the doors, Squeak…. squeak followed by a rattling of the handles again. There was no way those doors were not locked this time, I had even pushed on them to make sure, they had not budged, so I knew they could not just open by themselves. Jumping out of bed, my heart thumping out of my chest, looking out the window as before, but again nobody was there, It was still dark, there was no security light on this time and I could just about see that gate at the bottom of the garden was still securely shut, there was nobody in the garden, This time I went marching to the kitchen, somebody had to be messing with me, I was fuming. I flicked the lights straight on and could not believe what I was seeing, yet again both doors were wide open, I just stood and stared at them. It was a beautiful night, no wind, nothing I could not get my head around it. Now angry, angry that it was doing this to me when I was on my own, in a rage now I shouted: "Do not touch my f****ing doors again".

I pulled them too, did all the checks that I had done before, and came back to bed but this time I went and woke Jack up, and asked him if he would come and sleep in my bedroom as I was scared and needed someone near me, he reluctantly and mumping all the way, came in, He had also mentioned how much he wanted to move, He got on the blowup mattress we had bought for camping a couple of years ago.

All lights were off now so Jack could go back to sleep.

So happy to see it was finally getting lighter outside. At this stage I was so tired, I felt sick, I was that tired, but still not daring to go to sleep in case the doors opened again.

I then started hearing voices, there seemed to be more than one voice, and my adrenaline started to kick in. There was definitely someone downstairs.

Picking my phone up and quickly getting ready to call the police, I saw that it was just after 4.30 am. Then hearing Jack whisper "Mum, can you hear that?" Thinking he was asleep I did not realise he'd been listening. Answering him "Yes, what do you think it is?", he said "it sounds like someone is having a conversation downstairs, phone grandad," It was not the time to laugh but I gave out a big chuckle.

There was no way my dad was being called to come up and tackle whoever was in this house at this hour of the morning.
Explaining to him why we may have to phone the police instead, he got very scared. This was one time I was not able to protect him from all this.
Something was in our house and had been playing games with me all night.
It was coming from downstairs, that we knew, so both sitting up we looked towards the landing and saw the TV light was on downstairs. "Jack, please come with me", I asked, Hating myself for having to get him in the middle of all this but needing some support, we then made our way to the top of

the stairs, I gave him my phone and told him to get ready to dial 999, he stood there looking so scared and nervous whilst I slowly went down a step at a time, taking the 3rd step I leaned forward and could see that the tv was on.
Walking further down, taking one step at a time I reached the bottom. The dining room doors were still bolted shut.
Looking around to make sure there was nobody in there I then shouted up to Jack to tell him it was ok and that we were safe, finding the remote I quickly turned the TV off and ran back up the stairs.
 We were both visibly scared and now I felt even more guilty for waking Jack up in the first place. Looking back, I do not think I could have stayed in this house that night had he not been at my side.

To this day the doors have never opened on their own again. I think "FRED" was telling me he hated all the change. Jack did ring his grandad up, telling him what had happened.

Mum and Dad yet again told us to get in the car and come sleep at theirs and yet again we did not. Absolutely no way I was going to let him drive us out of our home. We settled back down to try and get a little bit of sleep, me now assuring Jack that everything was fine, telling him that I must have left it on by mistake. He needed to feel safe so I'd rather him think it was me than be scared and think it was "Fred."

He seemed to settle for this explanation, telling me from now on he'd turn the TV off, he was making me feel like a child, but this was better than him being frightened in his own home so I just took the scolding, all the while trying to wrap my head around the events that had just happened.

The time the TV had switched on was exactly 4.40 am. I knew this because I had picked my phone up seconds after we had first heard the voices.

That night we were so very close to dialling 999.

There are countless little incidents, I cannot even recall all of them—cold breezes, shadows, electronics turning on and off, appliances blowing up (kettles, hair dryers, straighteners, you name it, it has popped, banged or burnt) even though there was nothing wrong with them, some brand new. Just two days ago, while I was typing this book, Jack came running downstairs to me, I asked, "What's up?" He looked annoyed and said, "Where is Annie? You said we'd have a peaceful day today. Why are the kids here? Confused, I replied, "Nobody's here, Jack, it's just me and you, what are you on about?" He then explained that he had heard Annie calling him, telling him to hurry up and come downstairs. Explaining to him that there was nobody else but us in the house and myself not hearing a word, he looked at me dumbfounded.

I got the "Why are you trying to scare me, Mum? It is not funny. Stop it."

He was so spooked by this that he refused to go back upstairs, leaving me to go up and turn off his gaming console, all the way keeping my head down and being as quick as possible.

He spent the rest of the afternoon glued to my side until his dad got home, Roger had to bribe him and reassure him for quite a while before he finally caved in, His dad had to go up with him through and game for a couple of hours until he felt safe again.

What people who have not experienced this sort of thing do not get is that you have to carry on, you cannot just drop everything and run. It becomes a private battle. You are battling with air; it is an impossible situation to be in.

There is no way you would let a stranger come and drive you out of your home, you would fight both tooth and nail for it, that is all I am still trying to do.

Chapter 11- THE DOG.

We got Jack a dog when he was 5 years old because we thought he was lonely. There were only him and Lee at home now, and Lee was always out playing football with his mates or going to football practice or matches with Andy.
He was also going to college, so he was out quite a lot.
He missed the house being full, he had loved the weekends when Mum, Dad, the kids, and their partners would all come around for a Sunday lunch, that was when he was at his happiest.
 I found out that someone I knew was selling some Lhasa Apso puppies, Lee came with me to go see them, My friend also had a pig, it was huge, apparently, she had

bought this pig thinking that it was a micro pig but soon found out that this was not the case, she was like a guard dog, slept under the stairs at night and what we soon where to find out was that she had taken a shine to what was soon going to be our pup.

Lee was the one to pick him, watching him look over all the beautiful puppies. I suddenly saw him gravitate towards one of the smallest ones, he was snuggled up next to the pig.

The pig thing sealed the deal, I think. We all fell in love with him straight away, we chose the name Parker, and it suited him perfectly. Those first few nights he slept in my bed on a blanket that I'd put on my chest, he never cried once, we had rubbed the blanket on his mommy when going to get him and it had helped settle him straight in, with not one bit of bother.

Over those first few years of being here, Parker has had us all scratching our heads, wondering what it was that he could see, and we could not. We have a picture of Parker lying on the end of the sofa asleep, something is floating above him, it has wings and you can see bent legs dangling next to his head, There have been times when we have been sat watching TV and then all of a sudden he has jumped up and started barking at the bottom of the stairs sometimes doing circles and sometimes growling.

There was never anything or anybody there, He'd make us all jump in the process.

We would all shout for him and try getting him to come sit with one of us, to try and calm him down.
He is so protective of the babies he puts his backside towards their bodies and looks away as if to say, "Come near them I dare you" It is an extremely cute, but also a reassuring, protective thing to see him do.
One day when Jack was at school and Lee was at college, I was standing ironing at the bottom of the stairs. I saw him jump off the chair he had been lying on. Watching him I saw him look towards the dining room, he then started to growl, his hair all stood up on end, and his tail had gone down. Looking at where he was growling there was nothing there, he was growling into thin air, I could not see anything, He then

went ballistic, something was upsetting him and there was nothing I could do.

Trying to shout him over to me he was taking no notice, his stature still frozen and facing the same direction, barking and snarling still when suddenly a freezing gust of wind went straight past me, I actually felt it go past my ear making my hair go onto my face and as this happened Parker came running past and followed it up the stairs, barking and growling as he did.

He came straight back down but still kept on growling, all the while looking up the stairs, he stayed there for a couple of minutes still looking up then he just stopped, he took one final look up again turned himself around, and jumped back on the chair he had been on before this had all happened, he then put his head down and dozed off like nothing had ever happened.

I then moved my ironing board into the kitchen and carried on from there.

The barking at fresh air is still to this day and they come on for no reason at all unless he sees a cat or a squirrel passing the window, He also goes crazy if someone comes to the door.

Many times, he has seemed scared and growled at space but there is nothing we can do, He normally follows you around and does not seem to settle when he is like that,

The time the doors opened, he did a soft growl downstairs, He hadn't gone ballistic that time but something was rattling him, He had come upstairs and id tried to get him up onto the bed but he would not come, we had watched him put his back to us and faced the door like he used to with the babies, he would let a small growl sound now and again until it was all over, We know he must have seen something.

There is nothing worse than seeing and hearing that dog just go off, we have jumped out of our skins, swore, spilled tea, and shouted at him for it and we know it is not his fault, but when it is quiet and you've just been chilling as it happens I think it would be anyone's reaction.

I am sure he laughs at us when he does this.

CHAPTER 12 - PROOF

Many times, I have seen shadows go past the archway or a door. The landing on the top of the stairs seems to be a major hotspot so I decided to try and capture some kind of evidence.
knowing that 4.40 was the time most things happened I thought if I was awake before that time I'd placed my camera on the cove at the top of the stairs facing it towards my bedroom door to see if "FRED" eventually would make an appearance.
It was a couple of nights later and just before 4 am I woke up and went downstairs to make myself a cup of coffee. It was a winter morning, horribly cold and very dark outside. I had checked as

soon as I woke up to see if the heating were on, but the radiator was freezing.
suddenly remembering that I had set the system to come on at 5 am.
 That would get the house warmed up for when Jack would be getting up for school, but it was too cold today to wait.
 Getting it all sorted and changing the timer, not taking a bit of notice of the cold, the heating then switched on.
The windows were frosted over, and I was breathing smoke with my breath all the way back upstairs, but because it was a chilly morning I did not even think it could be something else, it had been so quiet lately.
I went back to my bedroom and wrapped my duvet up to my neck to try and get some warmth.

Putting the TV on, I started to watch something. Checking my phone so that at 4.30 am I would place my phone in the cove that was at the top of the stairs.

I was into whatever I was watching because I nearly missed the moment, I looked, and it was 4.34 am. I jumped out of bed and put my phone on record, then went back to watching my program. I left the phone there for a while and checked the program to see how long there was left. It said 17 minutes, I then knew it must have gone past the 4.40 am time slot.

Getting out of bed and going to retrieve my phone I climbed back into bed.

I cannot tell you how scared I was and what it took that morning to view that footage.

I sat all alone and had no idea as to what I had captured.
All I do know is that on my first attempt, I had captured "FRED" and the time he had walked past my doorway was exactly 4.40 am.

That video was sent to my family and close friends, The morning it had happened on the video you see a dark shadow with a glow around it fill in the gap in my bedroom door, it was just for a second but the light that had always been there from a plug safety light was gone whilst he passed, when you have your door half open / closed you have a small gap between the door frame and door and because it was so dark I had left the bathroom light on, just left that door slightly open so just a chink of light also was allowed through, the camera would not be able to video total darkness, its a brilliant catch and a few days later I put the camera against my wardrobe door, this time to try and capture it from a different angle and at exactly 4.40 am there he was again, this time you could see his frame, he was very well built like the last time I had seen him. He was black and you could see the shape of his head, a big round head, He had wide-set shoulders, I could not see anything below his chest it was just his top half that caught my attention.

I did not do any more videos after that as I now knew I had all the evidence I needed; it freaked me out a bit to know that he was walking around upstairs in the mornings whilst we were all sleeping.

There have been quite a few pictures I have captured now.

There is one of Jack and his friend Noel, and at the side of Noel there is a bright light, It is next to his face but they are all the same, Another picture was taken on Halloween, We always go overboard with the trimming of the house, every year saying "I'm not doing this next year the kids are too old now" but every year we trim the house back up.

At some point, I must have gone outside to take a picture of the window. It looked so nice with the carved pumpkins and flickering candelabra.

Jack had seen me go out, he had climbed on the sofa and was looking out at me in his fancy dress costume, so I had quickly taken a picture of him. When we looked at the pictures the next day there was visibly an arm around Jack's shoulder. It was bright and reminded me of what had happened when he was a baby, The time he was guided into our bedroom. It was the same shape and the same colour.

The next picture was also on Halloween weekend this time Jack had friends over to go trick or treating, I also had a couple of friends over, Mum and Dad, and the older kids were there as I do hotdogs and burgers and put on a bit of a spread, One of his besties Rae had on a zombie outfit, her face all gruesome and made up, she looked fantastic, Jack had on a Slenderman outfit, they are stood side by side in the dining room, I took a snap and in the middle of them on the photo is something blurry, you can't see their hands, A bright light is there merging their hands, the next picture seconds later is just fine.

There are lots of videos earlier on when Jack was little of "orbs" flying around him, there is one of him in bed asleep and a mist above him.

One where he is innocently playing his guitar and A orb flies by in front of him, you see him follow it with his eyes.

I have not been able to catch the fast shadows in the dining room because, by the time I have managed to get my phone out, they have gone.

I recently asked my daughter if she'd let me borrow her old baby monitor. We want to place it on the stairs they are supposed to be great for capturing things.

The most recent evidence is when I was in the garden watching my grandson play, he is two and a half, Just sitting at the table with a coffee in my hand, The sun was out, it was a beautiful day, and I had set up his water table and put his dinosaurs in the sand side and his boats and sharks in the waterside, he was singing away whilst throwing the sand into the water and making a good old mess when I looked up at my bedroom window.

Then my eyes moved over towards Jack's window that was situated above the garage, Now squinting as I could see someone looking at me, In that split second my heart skipped a beat, There plain as day was a man staring back at me, I could not take my eyes off him, slowly reaching for my phone whilst still looking at him I went to put it in camera mode, My eyes left him for a split second then as quickly as I could I pointed it up to the window and snapped a picture.

Looking down at my phone I gasped, I caught him.

When I looked back up, he had gone, that's when a thought came to me, maybe it's one of the kids, they must have come in and not said anything.

I always lock the door when I am in the garden, Jack was at school and the older ones were all at work but thinking id go check to make sure I got up and made my way to the house, I went into every room, and there was no one to be seen, I also checked the front door to make sure it wouldn't have even been a stranger that may have just walked in. The door was locked, the keys still in the door.

I have shown that photo to quite a lot of people, all can see the top half of a man.

CHAPTER 13 - ATTENTION

Me and Roger were sitting downstairs trying to watch a quiz show on TV.
 Earlier in the week Mum had bought me a lovely fake green plant for my new kitchen, It was an ivy look one, It dangled over the side of my new cupboards giving a nice green fresh look, it had been on top of this corner cupboard now since receiving it, on walking into the kitchen to go check on the tea Id opened the oven door, on doing this the plant came flying off the top of the cupboard, There is no way It could have fallen that far, It was right into the middle of the kitchen floor, It had just missing my head.

Roger had shouted out "What was that?" I just made some other excuse for the noise as I was not going to acknowledge "FRED" today.

Carrying on with the tea and turning a blind eye to what had just happened, Jack then came running into the kitchen, he was mumbling how he was fed up with us calling his name, "Why don't you just come and tell me once instead of shouting my name over and over", His dad, who had followed him into the kitchen looked at me, We both said at the same time "Jack, we have not shouted you once you must be hearing things", Jack replied but "I heard you mum stop messing me about". We had not called him once, but he would not listen to us.

Still trying to ignore "FRED," we finished tea, and I came upstairs to run a bath, after the events of today It was so needed, Taking a wine with me and my book.

  Roger and Jack had taken the dog for his evening walk to a nearby lake like they always did when he was home.

Knowing that the door would be locked and they would be gone for an hour or so, I settled into the bath, Suddenly I had a feeling that someone was watching me, looking around there was nobody there, The atmosphere changed something was definitely in here with me, Then that all too familiar breeze went past my head, now knowing very well who it was, I thought to myself "Just ignore him, do not let him ruin your bath" laying back down I started to wash my hair.

There was a penguin toothbrush holder that had been in the same place on the side of the sink for years, suddenly It flew off the side of the sink, smashing down onto the floor.

That was me up and out of the bathroom, still not letting him get the better of me and still adamant that I was not going to acknowledge him I went downstairs.

My hair was wrapped in a towel and not yet rinsed properly I walked into the kitchen, my hair still had soap in it so going to the kitchen sink I finished it off there. Glancing at the kitchen clock after id only had ten minutes in the bath.

I was so mad with "FRED", but still had my mind set on ignoring him.

After mustering the courage to go back upstairs and hearing the lads coming back in the door, I now felt a little bit braver.

Plugging in the hair dryer and sitting on the end of my bed, I smelt burning, looking down at the hair dryer I saw sparks flying out at the back of it,

Quickly reaching down to unplug it a big "POP !!" exploded, It had blown up in my hands, I chucked it across the room and shouted in my temper, "Pxx Off FRED", I could hear the lads laughing downstairs, Jack saying to his dad 'Why is she shouting at "FRED ?"'.

"FRED" had won yet again.

Nothing else happened for a while after that.

CHAPTER 14 - JUMPY

One of the things now is that I am very jumpy.

One of the kids could just innocently walk into a room and I would scream or jump out of my skin.

A few years ago, I was just brushing my garden decking down. It was a beautiful summer day, and I was trying to make the garden look nice for the weekend because we had decided to host a BBQ for the family. Brushing away in a world of my own, just getting on with it when Jo, next door, popped her head over the fence to say hello.

The scream I let out was loud, far too loud and my heart skipped a beat, she started to laugh, then apologized. "Take it you have had a "Fred" morning," she said.

The morning had been a strange one and that was one of the reasons for me being outside.

In the bathroom earlier cleaning, I was on my hands and knees trying to reach as far as possible under the bath, the day before Grace and baby Gray had been. They always went home fed and bathed.

Their Mum and Dad worked long hours we liked to send them home all ready for bed.

Toys were everywhere, it had been a splash nightmare but they had loved it. After picking most of the toys from around the bath there were just a couple under the bath I could not reach.

The next morning a kid's plastic sword was my secret weapon to knock the toys towards me so I could grab them and put them back into the toy box we kept at the side of the bath.

On the last action figure I could see, I stretched my arm out as far as I could and managed to whack it towards me, feeling that I had won the battle, reaching to pick it up, it spun around and slid to the side of me, there was no water on the floor and I was on my stomach my legs stretched behind me, knowing I'd not knocked it with anything as looking the sword was still at the side of me.

Wondering if it had just been slippery and trying not to read too much into it, I Got off the floor and bent down to pick it up, it then slid slowly back under the bath.

Watching it go in slow motion I just stood looking at it move. Then a cold breeze went past my ear and that was it, I legged it downstairs and out into the garden.

Jo was so sorry for scaring me, it had not been her fault it is just that I had my guard up.

Neighbours/ friends have knocked on the door before and if I was in another room or had gone upstairs for something, not knowing they had already knocked, then they had let themselves in and on coming into the room I was in had caused me to give out a scream and nearly have a heart attack. It makes others laugh but it is no fun for me.

Footsteps are what we hear a lot of, and they unnerve me, but they are a lot better than when I hear the other steps, the animal ones, it is not human feet that is for sure, more like pads or hoofs.

Sitting in the room on my own for a change, no kids, or grandkids I was enjoying some me time, having just finished off the housework I made myself a drink and put the TV on. It must have been an hour into whatever had been on when I heard a pitter-pattering coming from the kitchen, It sounded like something was running around in there, it was running fast and like it was chasing something, there was no flooring on at this time, as we were in the middle of doing the kitchen, It had been bare for a few weeks now. Looking across to the sofa where Parker our Dog was laying, I knew it was not him; I got up thinking something had got in from the outside. Walking towards the kitchen not knowing what I was about to find I opened the doors, The noise stopped straight away.

 I looked all the way around, but nothing was there. Closing the doors and making my way back into the living room, a big crash came from the kitchen. Opening the doors again and looking at what I could see, now on the floor was the rubber plant my mum had bought me a few weeks earlier, going over to it and picking it up I placed it back on top of the cupboard.

I walked back into the room and sat back down, this plant had fallen before I recalled, the day Mum had given it to me, we had both witnessed it being thrown off the shelf. Mum and I had laughed about it at the time.

The pitter-pattering had me baffled, there was nothing there, so there was nothing I could do.

 Picking up the remote and starting to watch the rest of whatever It was that I'd been watching, I heard it again, The pitter-pattering but this time it was on the stairs landing just above me, turning off the TV I jumped up, shouted at the dog to come with me and started walking very fast towards the door.

 As I reached the door there was an almighty crash and it came from the kitchen, there was no way I was going back in there to find out what it was this time.

The rest of the day I spent with my mum and dad.

Coming home after picking up Jack from school later that day, walking into the kitchen there was the plant on the floor.

We still have that plant, and it has never fallen since, it is in the same place as it has always been.

Talking to friends and neighbours they have recounted a few events that have happened over the years that I have either forgotten or rather tried to forget, one friend reminded me the other day of the strange phone call that I received years ago and to be honest, it has surprised me that this had not been mentioned on my storytelling before because it was a scary experience.

On a day out with a friend Clare, Jack, and her two kids, Rae and Neil, We were sat talking, The kids were happily paddling in the nearby stream, getting soaked, It was a beautiful hot summer day plus it was the school holidays, We somehow in our conversation got on to the topic of "Fred".

Something had happened when she had been in the house the weeks before. We both do not remember what she had witnessed, but she had witnessed something. I had been telling her that he had been incredibly quiet. It had been a lovely time for the past couple of weeks when my mobile phone started to ring, and a withheld number appeared.

As a rule, I never pick up these calls, but for some reason this time I did. Putting the phone to my ear an almighty screeching sound came out, it was so loud, looking across she was looking at me, her eyes wide with confusion, Clare had heard it also. Throwing the phone on the mat we were sitting on, we both sat in silence before I said, 'let us not talk about "Fred" anymore'. We nervously laughed but both agreed that the subject was now closed.

Yes, it could have been anything, I admit that, but the timing was eerily spot on.

So many silly things let me know that he is here but letting me know he's here is his thing.

There are many times that I have had to look to see if the dog was in the bedroom. Those animal footsteps are awful, they are loud as well. I shouted the dog's name, only for him to come bounding upstairs, proving it could not have been him.

The wardrobes in my room creak and shut at silly times in the mornings, The kid's bedroom wardrobes do their own thing as well. Knocking on most walls is a common thing to happen. My eyes dart towards the noises, all the while hoping not to see anything. My stomach always drops, wondering what is coming next.

CHAPTER 15 - Footsteps

There are days when it is so quiet, peaceful and you know that there is nothing here, the air is lighter in the house and I do not tend to be as jumpy, but after these kinds of days, it was like it was saving up its energy because it would always do something bigger and even though we were used to it happening when it did happen it still scared the hell out of me, as you never knew what was coming next.

This particular month had been fairly quiet and life had carried on as normal, this one Wednesday morning I was in the living room watching my catch-up programs when something caught my eye from the direction of the dining room, the shadow, went slowly this time, it went from the left of the archway to the right, passing straight through the wall towards my neighbour's house, thinking" here we go again "on knowing we had been lucky this month and instinctively bracing myself for what was about to happen.

The dread that you feel when it starts back up is horrendous, getting up to make myself a drink, again taking myself out of the room, on returning with my drink, and sat on the sofa, the open staircase behind me, when I heard a door slam shut upstairs.

Knowing which door it was, as always it was Annie and Jack's old bedroom door, Then I heard footsteps on the landing, really loud and plodding, then as quickly as they had started, they stopped.

Turning my head slowly towards the stairs and not able to see and not able to see anything I went back to what I had been watching, then that all too familiar freezing breeze came whizzing past me. Quickly sitting up, my head turned towards the stairs again, my eyes went towards the top steps and that is when I saw them, a pair of boots, they were light brown in colour, standing still on the second step as though they were coming down.

I jumped up and shouted for the dog who was in the garden to come. On hearing me he pounded towards me and after quickly scooping him up I ran straight round to Jo's house petrified and wondering whose feet had just been seen.

Jo had after calming me down, come back round with me an hour or so later, we did a sweep of the house, my phone already having dialled 999 ready to be pressed. That incident also scared me. Now I refuse to look up towards the stairs from the sofa.

Lying in bed a few nights later and trying to sleep, I felt the bed move like someone had walked into it, In my head I thought straight away that it was Jack, he often banged into the corner of the bed if he had been searching for his phone charger, I always borrowed it, but he normally chuntered when coming to retrieve it, there was no chuntering so I sat up to see if it was Jack.
There was nobody there, Then I heard shuffling coming from the

bottom of the bed, grabbing the remote that I had placed beside me earlier. I pressed the TV on. It gave me immediate light, my eyes adjusted quickly to the sudden change, and then thought "It is just the dog," gently pulled the covers back and kneeled up, my eyes trying to peer over the end of the bed, hoping to find Parker sleeping, but there was nothing there. I know very well that something had just been there, there was no way it could have gone from that area that quickly.

I slowly laid back down, picked the tv remote back up, and turned the volume off, no way was the tv being turned off. I needed light. Getting myself settled and just dropping off again, it went ice cold, all down the right side of me. It was freezing, even though there was a quilt cover and a big throw over on top of me. Pulling the quilt up towards my neck and angrily muttering "F*** off FRED!". No sooner had the words left my lips, than that freezing feeling lifted, and it was back to normal again. That night was yet another sleepless night, the TV was left on till the next morning.

Only yesterday morning I was on my hands and knees cleaning the bathroom floor when hearing what sounded like footsteps coming towards me, the bathroom has a bit of a walk that opens up into a large open space, Instantly thinking it was Jack I said, " Jack give me a minute please I've nearly finished " There was no reply, Looking up I saw that nobody was there, Trying to ignore whatever had just come into the bathroom I just carried on.

Chapter 16 - Here To Stay

Over the years people have said, "Why do you stay there," or "I would be gone, "and even remarks calling me" stupid " for staying, what they do not understand is that this is" MY HOME", Not "FREDS" and who is to say that " FRED" would not follow us if we moved to another house?.

If this was guaranteed we would be out of here in a shot.

When it all first started happening, I didn't want to leave, nobody wants to be scared in their own home and nobody wants their kids to be scared either, it became a battle of the wills, and now as much as I would like to say we are used to

the goings on, we are not. More like putting up with them. It has become the norm, there is not one thing we like about "FRED."
He is here to stay. We might as well get used to it.
Things happen for days and then nothing for weeks, there are no set days when we can say," FREDs" here, as we just do not know.

Recently my Dad was changing a light fitting in the kitchen and he had asked me to turn all the electrics off, The electrical box was situated under the stairs in a little cupboard behind the sofa, on pulling the sofa out to get to the box, sticking my head in the cupboard, I switched the whole set of switches off, just to be safe, on getting back up and going back into the kitchen I watched my dad

testing the electrical items he needed.
He turned the microwave on, but it did not work, then he tried switching the kitchen light on and that too did not come on.

Watching him climb up the ladder and start to unscrew the light fitting that needed to be changed, all a sudden, we heard a click, looking to where the sound had just come from, we realised it was the kettle, it had lit up and had started to boil. We both just looked at each other, shaking his head at me and getting down the ladder, he said, "Are you trying to finish me off, lady".
I looked at the now-boiled kettle and said, "Dad!, I promise, I turned it off, let me show you", we went into the living room, and Dad got

down onto his knees to see for himself, as you could tell he did not believe me when the familiar phrase that he is known for came booming out of the cupboard "JEEEEAAAZZZZUUSSS" !!, the electricity was off, we had no idea how the kettle had been able to boil itself as there was no electricity supplying it

Later that same day when everyone had gone, it was just me and Jack and Roger.
Jack was sitting on the sofa with his earphones in watching something on his mobile phone, we had just finished tea and he was chilling.
Roger had gone outside to fetch the washing in from the line.
 I had started clearing the dining room dishes away taking what I

could carry and popping them into the sink, All of a sudden that too-familiar cold breeze flew by me, There were no doors or windows open, I just knew something was about to happen, that dreaded feeling came over me and as I always do at first, I tried to ignore it.

I came back from the kitchen to get the last lot of dishes and that's when I looked towards Jack who, thank God, was engrossed in whatever he was watching, when I saw it.

What I saw was a shadow pass from one side of the archway to the other, it moved slowly this time not like when I had seen them before, they had just whisked by really fast and just been caught, this time though it went in slow motion, it did not have a human shape, it was like a big black mass with a faded grey colour around it, I just stood there for a few seconds rooted to the spot, watching it go from one side to the other until it just floated into the bottom of the stairs cupboard. Trying to ignore what had just been seen I carried on collecting the rest of the dishes. On turning around to walk back into the kitchen another breeze zipped past my ear.

 I thought "please don't appear this close to me" I was a little bit scared now, having just seen something dark, it had also been a big shadow.

 It had been few feet away from me but something was now in the kitchen with me and being alone with it unnerved me, I kept my head looking forward, muttering to myself, "ignore it, just ignore it", when some tools that my dad had left on the kitchen side started to rattle, it was not a big noise but I could definitely hear that they was being touched and there was only me in the kitchen at this time and it was not me , placing the dishes in the sink I walked very fast ,back towards the dining room ,just getting to where the double doors are when all of a sudden something hit the back of my leg on my calf , it felt like I had been bitten it really stung me, looking back to see what had just hit my leg, there was a screwdriver on the floor, Just beside my foot I ran into the room, sat on the sofa and pulled up my left trouser leg, there was a angry red mark but it had not pierced my skin, It could have been so much worse, I was so mad, this was not good at all, I did not say a word to anyone, Jack had not moved in all of this.

Rubbing my leg and trying to find the courage to go back into the kitchen I got back up. Went into the kitchen, picked up the screwdriver, and moved all the tools into a nearby drawer.

From that day to this when having any work done all tools have to be moved straight away. I do not know why, "FRED" hates it when we do anything to the house, one lady that I had gone to see told me to always ask for permission before doing something in the home or tell him what you are doing and why you are doing it, so that is what I have now started to do, to be fair since starting to do this there has been no more of the throwing of the tools. A little safer at least.

I have tried just about everything to help him on his way, to get him to pass over but nothing has ever worked, my son had his mates over a few months ago and they wanted to know about "FRED", one of the lads mum must have told him what I had posted on a social media forum, he had asked numerous times for me to tell them about "FRED", Jack had not known the full ins and outs as we had always kept as much as we could from him, not wanting him scared in his own home, he was also asking for me to tell them a few stories.
I did eventually give in and shared a few with them in the end but not the really bad experiences, Jack had to sleep in his room at night after all and we did always try to keep as much from him as possible. He was now a lot older

after all. I also showed them a picture and soon realised that this had been a huge mistake. We had a really challenging time getting him to go upstairs alone for a few days after, I did then try to tell him that "FRED" had now gone but he did not believe that either.

Chapter 17 - Other Recollections

The following month we were all in the room, the grandkids, Grace and Gray were playing with their toys, we were all chattering away and then I saw a dark shadow pass over Grace, knowing nobody else had seen it as not one person had said anything, I watched it carefully and then saw her shiver, knowing she must have felt something.
Gray then came to take something from her, and I watched him look at the wall in front of him and go running to his daddy.
All the while I did not say a word. I did not want to scare any of them or make a big thing of it. but I saw what had just happened and thought to myself "Oh no! Not my babies, please leave them alone ".

These last few weeks have been hit-and-miss, it is now either all or nothing.

It was the school holidays, earlier in the day I had taken Jack to my Mum and Dad's house so he could stay with them for a few hours. Today I was not feeling too good so I wanted to get back home as soon as I could and get some rest. Andy was taking Jack to see the new Marvel film later that afternoon so that was going to give me a few more extra hours to rest also.

  I nipped to the shops on the way back so that I would not have to go back out, after lugging the four carrier bags from the car, when I had finally managed to open the door and take the shopping into the kitchen putting the bags onto the side quickly as it had just started to rain went to fetch the now dry washing in off the line, It had been outside since 6 am that morning so not wanting to have to rewash it all thought I'd just go and fetch it in. Then folding it on the dining table and taking it upstairs.

On reaching the top of the stairs I just stood still.

Seeing that every single door upstairs was wide open, knowing for sure that each and every one had been shut before going out earlier that morning. I had always done this so that the dog could not get onto the beds, plus all the windows were wide open as it had been a beautiful hot day before the rain had started.

I went around the upstairs shutting all the doors again, trying to figure out if it had just been me forgetting to do it that morning, also doubting myself yet again. Then I made my way downstairs to put the shopping away.

I had made myself a special juice earlier that morning, getting it out of the fridge I made my way upstairs, willing myself into doing the ironing, thinking if I did a little at least then that would be ok.

 I had only been at it say 15 minutes before realising that I had left my juice canister in the bathroom, so on going to retrieve it I came back onto the landing when I felt a lovely cold breeze, it was welcomed as if I'd already said, it had been a very hot day.

Not once did my thoughts go towards "FRED."

Then on looking across the landing, I saw it yet again.

The box room door was wide open, There was no way it could have just opened by itself, That door was a nightmare to open without it making a sound, I had heard nothing, It had to be shoulder barged to get through sometimes and the door handle was stiff, It took some real strength to open, going over to the door I then closed it, Slamming it shut to make sure it was closed this time when hearing a creek I looked back over my shoulder, towards the door I had just closed, then seeing the door slowly open again I turned to my bedroom and started to iron, ignoring what I had just seen.

Later that same day I had done all that needed to be done, I had gone around all the rooms putting the ironing away and shutting the windows, my dad had rung me and said there was going to be a storm later that evening. Jack and Andy were still at the cinema, Andy was taking him out for a burger after the movie then going to the amusement arcade and would not be back for a couple more hours and my husband was working away this week so it was just me.

I was really tired, felt ill and very hot and bothered, I could not wait to have a bath, so on going into the bathroom and putting on the taps, I stupidly thought to myself that this was going to be a lovely relaxing hour, going downstairs to check all the doors were locked, I went to the refrigerator and took out a very cold bottle of wine and poured myself a large glass, taking it back to the bathroom, I also had a good book that my friend Sharon had fetched round earlier in the week, I was nearly halfway through the book and had wanted to try and finish it off, so getting the book from my bedside table taking it into the bathroom.

I was now in the tub and having a lovely chill, I had my book in my hand and the glass of wine at the side of the bath, there was no noise it was bliss, I had left the bathroom door open to let the steam out as it was a hot bath and I would not have been able to see my book if I had not done this, for some stupid reason I looked towards the box room door that was opposite the bathroom and watched it slowly open.

Getting the wine glass from the side of me, I took the biggest gulp, turned my head the other way, and carried on reading my book. Thinking it was a good idea to ignore him, I knew this would not end there.

The bedroom door then slammed shut.
I was out of that bath, dressed, and downstairs within five minutes.

Chapter 18 - Living Together

I am now getting good at turning a blind eye, sometimes though it is hard to do.

A few weeks ago, after having what I would like to call a lull in the house.

Things had been quiet for a few weeks; nothing had been happening for quite a while.

One night we were all in bed when I was woken by the feeling of something jumping on the bottom of my bed. I listened to what I then heard as not footsteps but more like an animal's pattering steps.

I then heard Jack scream out from his bedroom, Mum!!!!! Mum !!!!!, looking at the time on my phone as I rushed to go into him, it was 2:34 am and as I groggily trudged into his room expecting him to be having a nightmare, he was not, instead he was sat up, bolt right, visibly shaking with his night light switched on.

What is up I said? Mum something was growling in my ear, I shouted at it to leave me alone, it woke me up and nearly scared me to death but I shouted at it to leave me alone, go away and it just stopped. "Aww Jack, it was just a dream, don't worry you're fine".

"Mum, please don't ignore me. I know what I heard", I was trying to pacify him. I did believe him as I had heard that growl myself but Jack had never known about this as I did not talk about "Fred" in front of him.

Sitting at the side of him and settling him back down, trying to console him, saying he had beaten whatever it was in his sleep, as it had gone as soon as he had told it to go away, after a few minutes waiting for him to be ok, thinking of the pattering of feet that I had heard just a few moments before his screams, I also was scared, scared to go back to my room, for fear that whatever had just jumped on my bed may still be there, putting the lights on I went downstairs to make a drink, there was no way I was going back to sleep, it was going to be a very long day.

The very next morning as Jack emerged into the kitchen his first words were" Mum you do not realise how scared I was last night" if only he had known that I did realise, and again I felt guilty for staying in this house and putting him through all of this. Later that week I was running late for my hairdresser Kerry, she came to my house to do my hair, as normal, I had forgotten that she was coming so whilst I was at my mum and dad, she had rung me to ask where I was, she was waiting outside my house as I pulled into my driveway five minutes later, quickly getting out of my car and a million sorry,s for my forgetting again, we went into the house but as soon as the door was opened the dog came running up to us wanting to be fused, he normally fused as someone came in the door but the way he was crying and doing circles was different.

We then noticed the TV was on, knowing it had been switched off. When I went out. In my head I thought cheers "Fred" you have saved me a job.

Kerry, who had gone straight to put her bags down in the kitchen, shouted "Do you know your doors are wide open?" I know very well that they had been shut before leaving, as it had been raining so they had not been open that morning, only to let the dog out earlier on.

Kerry looked at me shocked, I laughed and said, "Welcome to my word you have witnessed it yourself now".

I have seen Kerry since I started writing this book and she's reminded me also of the time that she had turned her straighteners on in the dining room, Picking them up to use them she then noticed that they were no longer on, I had actually seen her do this as we were talking, I'd heard that beep they do letting you know they are heating up.

She then went to switch them back on but the switch was already up, trying them in another socket they did the beep like before, looking at me and shrugging her shoulders we got the hair dryer and tried that in the same socket, It started blowing straight away, We then took the straighteners back, plugged them in and the beep happened as before but this time they stayed on. We did not say a word to each other, we both knew who was playing games with us.

Dad came up the next day and checked that socket and there was nothing wrong with it.

We have two lights on the wall in the living room. Those lights are a nightmare. We had them checked numerous times because the little bulbs they take blow constantly. Now they are ordered in bulk. We have changed the fittings also but for some reason "Fred" hates them.

The dog had been ill for a few days, and we had rushed him to the vet after nearly losing him. He had to have surgery and it was touch and go for a while, but he pulled through.

We fetched him home a day later still very sore with stitches all over his back end, he was getting the full v.i.p treatment from us all and also getting lots of new presents from the older kids, we had placed a soft blanket on the bottom of my bed and had to carry him up and downstairs like a baby, we would carry him in the garden now and

then so he could do his business.
It was a Saturday morning, Roger had just fetched him back up onto the bed as no way was it my time to get up, settling himself back down, getting himself comfortable. I saw him close his eyes. Roger had fetched me a cup of tea and was leaving for work, it was around six am, and I was watching Catch Up, all the while stroking Parker's head, the program had ended and I was about to start watching something else when the bottom of the stairs door slammed open as though someone had fallen into it, Parker jumped up and the first time since his operation started

to bark, he then to my horror jumped off the bed, there was no way he could be stopped in time, fearing he had popped his stitches and quickly following him to the top of the stairs, all whilst shouting for Roger who id thought had come back home, maybe he had forgotten something, I was going to give him a piece of my mind for being so loud knowing very well the dog was ill, plus Jack was sound asleep.

Quickly scooping him up and after checking his stitches were still intact, I placed him back on his blanket, he laid back down straight away he was exhausted, then took myself downstairs to go give Roger a piece of my mind, looking to see where he was I went from room to room but no one was there, I remember now that id even shouted for him but still nothing. Then checking the door to see if it was still locked and yes it was, ringing Roger next and asking him if he had returned, but he was already at work so it could not have been him.

It happened a few days later at around the same time, this time Parker sat growling by the bottom of the stair's door. There was something he could see but I could not.

I even tried to entice him away from the door with a treat, but he was having none of it. He also had a growling moment by the archway later that same day. Again, nothing was there.

This has just happened to me and Jack, we are in December 2024.

Thinking that I had finished writing for this book only 24 hours ago "Fred" had other ideas.

We had gone up to bed just after 10 pm, Putting the TV on thinking I'd have half an hour wind down time.

Settling down, watching nothing I heard the kitchen cabinets rattling, sitting up and turning the TV volume down to hear better I realised it had stopped.

Laying back down I then heard Parker start to whimper

downstairs, getting a little spooked but thinking maybe he just needed to go outside I got out of bed and went to let him out.

Back upstairs now turning the TV off hoping that he would settle, Then the door downstairs went, the noise it makes lets me know that someone has come into the living room.

I then heard Parker crying, not quite knowing what to do I picked up my phone, getting myself ready to call the police if needed.

Then my next thought was "It's Roger or one of the kids".

Shouting down to see if this was the case but getting no answer, I started to get scared.

It was midnight and now realising it could be "Fred" up to his antics I got up and put the stairs light on trying to ignore him but feeling braver with it on.
Parker then came in and started to paw at the bed. It was obvious he was distressed; he was whimpering, and his tail was down.
I don't normally let him on the bed but if it meant that I'd get some peace tonight then I would let him get on, I patted him to get up.
Waiting to drop off to sleep, the cupboard doors in the kitchen started to creak and rattle, trying to still ignore it, and knowing there was nobody but me and Jack in the house I did not move.

I must have dozed off because the next thing was being woken up by the sound of someone running up the stairs and into my bedroom.

I screamed, Parker barked and jumped off the bed growling at the top of the stairs, My heart was pounding, and to say that I was scared is an understatement, Not knowing what to do I jumped out of bed and with my head down and Parker on my heels ran into Jack's room and shut the door. It is guilt then that takes over. I'd woken him up knowing he had school the next day, I was so angry with myself and "Fred" but being that scared there was nothing else for me to do.

Sleeping on his bean bag on the floor with Parker next to me I felt safer.
This night was one of the scariest and worst nights I had had in months.

These last few weeks I have ignored a few shadows, a mist, and footsteps in different rooms. I now think I am grateful that is all he is doing. I can cope with this stuff, but I do not want to see "FRED" ever again.
 So, for now, unfortunately, I leave you with my story, no certain conclusion or resolution, I just hope that we can find peace and learn to live together. I just do not want to see him again.

The sightings, the noises and the breezes still carry on to this day, something that is known is that he hates being left alone, the things ramp up a notch if I've been away for a day or more, We know there is something here, but there is nothing I, or anyone else, can do to stop them.

I have tried everything that I could, the vicar, The priest, and the mediums but nobody is able to get rid of whatever it is.

So, we must just carry on as normal, trying to ignore it, that is all we can do, who knows!! one day "FRED" may just leave.

Printed in Great Britain
by Amazon